James allowed himself to savor the thought of unraveling Sara King....

He wanted to find the chink that would give him the leverage he needed to enable him to persuade her to sell the house to him. He would be fair—more than fair, he decided—but he would get what he wanted in the end. And looking at Sara now, with her red hair, pale, flawless skin and those translucent green eyes that were guarded, but couldn't help shimmering with fire, James had a sudden, disconcerting feeling that he was going to enjoy his dealings with her.

Cathy Williams

HIS CONVENIENT MISTRESS

Bedded by...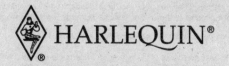

Blackmail

Forced to bed...then to wed?

HARLEQUIN®

TORONTO • NEW YORK • LONDON
AMSTERDAM • PARIS • SYDNEY • HAMBURG
STOCKHOLM • ATHENS • TOKYO • MILAN • MADRID
PRAGUE • WARSAW • BUDAPEST • AUCKLAND

ISBN 0-373-12479-1

HIS CONVENIENT MISTRESS

First North American Publication 2005.

Copyright © 2003 by Cathy Williams.

CHAPTER ONE

'YOU look tired, James. You work too hard. How many times have I told you that if you do not slow down, you will end up as another of those...those...?'

'*Statistics?*'

'And there you go. Making fun of me, an old woman who is only foolish enough to love you more than life itself.'

James's dark eyebrows flicked upwards in a teasing smile and he stretched out his long legs in front of him, crossing them at the ankles, cradling his glass of whisky with one hand.

Perfect. The perfect time of evening in the perfect place. The summer sun had turned into that warm amber glow that preceded the onset of twilight and outside was awash with the rise and fall of colour, every shade of green and yellow imaginable. This was wild Scotland at its most majestic. Through the massive windows, the landscape of the baronial estate unfolded into the horizon and the backdrop of mountains rose upwards into the sky like an implacable matriarch making sure that her feudal tenants kept to their place.

Ah, yes. Perfection. And, like all things perfect, it was really only palatable in small doses. A bit, James thought, like women. Too much of a good thing was guaranteed to dull the palate and bring on thoughts of boredom and restlessness.

'Are you listening to a word I'm saying, James Dalgleish?'

'With every ounce of attention, Mama.' He smiled lazily, sipped his whisky and focused on the handsome woman sitting on her upright chair by the fireplace, that was adorned, for summer, with a sumptuously large array of flowers, all hand-picked from the extensive gardens.

Maria Dalgleish, for all her talk about being an old woman, was an indomitable and youthful force, as untamed as the Scottish Highlands she adored, even after forty years of living in its towering purple shadows. The passion that coursed through her Italian veins had never quite abandoned her and she possessed a vitality he had never seen in a woman anywhere else in his life.

Perhaps, he thought idly, at the age of thirty-six he was a mama's boy, destined to become a cantankerous old man living alone in his sprawling mansion. But a cantankerous, *wise* old man, he thought, taking another appreciative sip of his drink. Wise enough to know from experience that women were drawn to money like moths to a flame. Better no woman than one of those. Although, better still, a series of women of conveniently abbreviated duration.

'Now, James, how long will this visit be? I hope you have not forgotten that you have duties here. Trevor wants to talk to you about some repair work to the roof and then there is the business of the summer party and there is no point grumbling about getting involved. It happens every year.'

'Did I say a word, Mama?'

'You do not have to. I can see the grumble in your expression.'

'I think I'll take a bit of a break this time, stay for a week or so before I fly to New York.'

'New York, New York. All this flying business every other day. It is no good for you. You are not a young man any more, you know.'

CATHY WILLIAMS 7

'I know, Mama.' He shook his head and adopted a penitent expression. 'I am ageing by the second and what I need to do is find a good woman to have a brood of babies and look after me.'

Maria huffed, tempted by the carrot offered to involve herself in one of those conversations dear to her heart, but it was getting late and she could tell from her son's expression that he was too relaxed to do anything other than humour her in that infuriatingly stubborn and relentlessly charming manner of his.

'Yes, well.' She clicked her tongue to imply that the subject would rear its head soon enough. 'Now, tomorrow evening the Campbells have asked us over for supper. Lucy is up from Edinburgh.'

'Oh, good heavens.'

'It will be very nice and you know how much everyone enjoys seeing you when you fly in.'

'I'm here to relax, Mama. Not get caught up in a hectic whirlwind of socialising.'

'Things are never hectic in this part of the world. And how will you ever meet a nice girl if you refuse to socialise?'

'I socialise in London. Too much, if you want to know.'

'But with the wrong sort of girl,' his mother muttered darkly, unperturbed by the impatient glitter in his eyes.

'Mama,' he warned, 'let's just leave this alone, shall we? Agree to differ? The girls I socialise with happen to be just what my jaded soul desires.'

'I will leave this alone, James, *for the moment,* although you are still too young to be jaded…it is late and besides…' Maria Dalgleish allowed her voice to trail off into speculative silence.

'Besides…what?'

'There is something you might be interested in…'

'It's…' James glanced at his sleek, expensive watch, and then looked drily at his mother '…nearly quarter to ten. Too late for mysterious guessing games.'

'Someone has moved into the Rectory.'

'What?' James sat up straighter, leaning forward to rest his elbows on his thighs. The lazy, indolent ease had been replaced by that watchful edge that his mother only occasionally glimpsed.

'Someone has moved into the Rectory,' Maria repeated, primly flicking invisible specks of dust from her flowered skirt.

'Who?'

'No one local. In fact, no one is quite certain…'

'Why didn't Macintosh tell me that the place had been sold? Dammit!' He stood up and began pacing the room, frowning as he contemplated his lawyer's crass inefficiency. He'd had his eye on the Rectory for the past three years, had used every ounce of his formidable persuasiveness to try and convince Freddie that he didn't need a place that big, that he would get way over the top if he chose to sell.

Freddie had always laughed, poured them both a whisky or three and explained that the lady was not up for grabs. That James's plans to convert the expansive Dalgleish estate into a first-rate hotel with his mother overseeing the details from the Rectory, which was ideally positioned alongside the estate, would just have to go on hold.

'I intend to live to a hundred,' he had said more than once, grinning wickedly at James's frustration, 'and when I do finally decide to go, maybe we can strike a deal. If you're still around, wee laddie. Though what I would do with the money is beyond me. I've no family to speak of to leave it to. Still, I'm not agin doing a favour for a neighbour. Especially one who is so desperate to bring jobs into this beautiful countryside of ours. Not to mention a bit of much needed glamour for our local lassies to get their bored teeth into.'

'Because it has not been sold,' Maria replied.

'I told the man a thousand times after Freddie died that I wanted the place. I'll have his hide for breakfast.' He paused to stare through the windows, frowning. Underneath all the bantering, Freddie had wanted him to have the place but, Freddie being Freddie, had died suddenly two months previously while driving his old banger to see if he could unearth something interesting at Loch Shiel and had left no will to indicate what he wanted done with the Rectory.

James had simply had to inform his solicitor in the town what *his* intentions were and it had not once crossed his mind that he would fail to get what he wanted once all the technicalities of the place had been sorted out. He had the money, could move with speed to tie up any annoying loose ends and would be doing a service to the community by converting his own rambling baronial manor into a hotel, not to mention taking care of his mother, who wasn't getting any younger and would be happier in the relative cosiness of the Rectory. Still close enough to keep a jaundiced eye on the manor, to argue with contractors and suppliers and employees, while not having to contend with the overwhelming size of the place. She didn't look her age, had still retained the pure bone structure of the model she had once been, but she was sixty-five and didn't need the worries of running a house the size of Dalgleish Manor with grounds to match, staff or no staff.

He was furious that his plans had been scuppered at the last minute. His mansion in the outer reaches of Scotland was there to soothe his harried spirits not harbour yet more stress that he could do without.

'Who's bought the place, then?' He spun round to look at his mother, switching on one of the table lamps to dispel the infernal duskiness that had settled in the room. 'Some speculator, I presume? Someone who wants to convert the place into a little bed and breakfast where he can fleece innocent tourists and hobnob with the local gentry?'

'You are not listening to what I have just told you, James.'

'Of course I'm listening! I've done nothing *but* listen since you dropped this little gem on me!'

'The place has not been *sold*,' Maria repeated emphatically.

'Not been sold? You just said…' He breathed a sigh of relief as his long-range plans began to once again take root in his head. He had already got Max, one of his top architects, to begin doing some preliminary work on the conversion of the manor, based on a series of photographs. Step two would be a trip to the place for a couple of weeks to see how viable his thoughts were.

'Well, if it's just a question of someone showing interest then that's fine. I was under the impression that the place was occupied.' He shrugged and shoved his hands into his pockets so that his trousers were dragged down slightly, the waistband dipping down the flat planes of his stomach. 'I can beat off any competitor.'

'Freddie left the Rectory to a relative,' Maria Dalgleish said bluntly.

'Freddie did…*what*?'

'Willed the place to a relative. Everyone was as surprised as you are.'

'He didn't have any living relatives.'

'Perhaps you could try telling that to the woman who moved in three days ago.'

'Woman?'

'I am not too sure what the relationship was. I do not even know what she looks like or how old she is. You can imagine that everyone is buzzing with curiosity.'

'Woman?' Why would a *woman* want to move to this part of Scotland? This was beautiful but rugged terrain, not the sort of place a woman would choose to make her home. His mother was one of the few women who had come to the area from afar and he knew from what she had told him smilingly over the years that she had arrived with a truckload of misgivings only to find that the rugged Highlands had suited her far more than she could ever have imagined. Jack Dalgleish had belonged to the place as much as the lochs and trees did and his happiness there had infected her—in fact had turned her into a pivotal member of the tightly knit community.

'No one is really even too sure what her name is.' Maria couldn't help savouring the mystery, even though she flushed sheepishly at her own nosiness. 'Valerie Ross happened to see the removal van heading out towards the Rectory and when she spoke to Graeme—you know Graeme—yesterday he told her that a woman would be moving in, but he couldn't speak. He was on his way out of the house to the airport and I am sure got a great deal of pleasure allowing Valerie to stew in her own curiosity.' Mother and son exchanged a split-second of mutual amusement at the accuracy of this surmise, then James was back to his frowning contemplation.

'A woman,' he murmured half to himself. 'Well, if she's decided to make this part of the world her bolt-hole, then she's either a sad little lady with no life to speak of, hoping to find one here, or else she's running away from something.'

'What nonsense.'

'Bad marriage, bad love affair, bad job.'

'And what will you do?' Maria looked at her son with a mixture of indulgence, down-to-earth cynicism and deep affection. 'Persuade her that it is in her best interests to sell the place to you?'

'Why not?' He hadn't realised, until this moment, how much he wanted to turn Dalgleish Manor into something, wanted the Rectory for his mother, wanted to invest some of his vast reserves of wealth and power in a project that was emotionally closer to home. His financial house, a place where deals and mergers were cemented and money made in sums only appreciative accountants could truly understand, kept him busy but it hadn't been enough. Wasn't that why he had trained his eyes on an ailing firm of architects and nurtured them into a multimillion-pound concern that now flourished throughout Europe? But the travel and privileges had done nothing for his soul. He *wanted* this project, wanted to watch it grow like a baby and delight in knowing that he would be doing what would eventually be right for his mother in the process. None of it would be possible without acquiring the Rectory. It was ideal.

A woman. He felt a slight stirring of interest at the prospect of getting what he wanted. A woman was a far different cry from Freddie or, for that matter, from someone looking to make a quick buck. A woman he could handle. Fairly, generously, magnanimously even.

'I think,' he said, stroking his chin thoughtfully, 'I might just pay a little visit to our new neighbour in the morning.'

'I hope you don't intend to intimidate anyone into doing anything,' his mother said sternly and he grinned at her, a devilishly winning grin.

'Now, now, Mama, would I?'

Intimidation would have been the sports car, garaged when he was away and pulled out whenever the weather put him in the mood to drive through the unsullied roads around the estate in a fast car with the top down.

Now, his old four-wheel-drive, on the other hand. Denim-blue, ten years old and still driving as sweetly as a nut. *That* wouldn't intimidate an agoraphobic spinster with a fetish for twitching net curtains. As he now thought of his mystery obstacle.

At ten o'clock the following morning he drove through his estate, breathing in the fine summer air wafting through the open windows, lush with the scents of grass and flowers and lochs, turned right when he hit the crossroads and took his time covering the short distance to the Rectory.

Sara heard the car long before she spotted it. Something to do with the utter absence of noise in the place, she supposed.

Yes, peace and silence had been things she had predicted weeks previously when she had sat at her glass kitchen table in her lavish apartment in Fulham, rereading the letter she had received from a solicitor whose name she had never heard, about a house in the wilds of nowhere willed to her by an uncle whose existence she had only dimly been aware of. Peace and silence that had seemed so alluring and were now proving to be unnerving, even after three days. Just something else unnerving to add to the list already mounting in the back of her mind. And unnerving was a kind way of putting it.

She waited by the kitchen window, watching the shimmering landscape and waiting to see the car that was almost certainly heading in her direction.

'Everyone will want to meet you,' she had been told slyly by Freddie's lawyer, when they had finally met face to face over a cappuccino in one of the trendy London cafés. 'They all pretty much expect the place to be sold.

As far as everyone was concerned, Freddie was alone in the world. No wife, no children, no family.'

Fool that she was, she had actually, six weeks ago, looked forward to the country life full of people who would know her name, had pleasantly anticipated walking into shops and chatting with the people inside them. Bliss, she had idiotically thought, after her time in London, where life had been lived at breakneck speed and smiling at the shop assistants was regarded as a form of lunacy.

Her three days of isolation and peace had put paid to her illusions. She hated it here, hated the lack of noise, hated the horizon-less countryside, hated the utter stillness and had avoided heading into the town with something approaching obsession.

Naturally, sooner or later, the town, she now thought, would come to meet her. One by one. And there, approaching in a blue vehicle, was visitor number one.

Oh, heavens, but she had made a dreadful mistake. She had dared to think that the grass was going to be greener on the other side, and greener it was here, yes. Literally. But that was as far as it went. *How on earth was she ever going to survive?*

The car trundled through the fields, wending a lazy and inexorable path towards the Rectory, and Sara fleetingly contemplated hiding.

Where was Simon? She listened, heard him in the snug across the landing from the kitchen, happy as a lark, setting up his bricks on the low wooden table no doubt, a handy, child-friendly piece of furniture, precious few of which had previously cluttered his life.

She only turned away from the window when the car was entering its final swing towards her circular courtyard. Then she breathed a little sigh of resignation, glanced briefly in the direction of the snug with an expression of longing and reluctantly opened the kitchen door.

She looked a mess. She knew that. In London, now a lifetime away, she had always been impeccably groomed. Had had to be, to compete in the heavily male-dominated world she had inhabited. Her long red hair had always been tamed away from her face, securely pinned up, her make-up had been the armour of the top businesswoman, as had her assortment of sober-coloured, extremely expensive designer suits. Snappy, fashionable, but not ostentatious. In the City, success was always subtly dressed.

Here, though, in the space of only a few days, her grooming had slowly but surely unravelled. No make-up for starters and certainly nothing approaching work clothes. Just jeans and T-shirts and flat loafers.

It was what she was wearing now. Faded jeans, snug-fitting dark green T-shirt that almost but not quite matched the colour of her eyes, and her brown loafers.

She stood by the kitchen door, squinting into the sun, barely able to make out the driver of the car.

Her hair was plaited back, one thick braid that fell almost to her waist, from which escaped the usual rebellious tendrils. An inelegant hairstyle but practical for the thousand and one jobs she had to do around the house.

Her visitor was a man. Sara shaded her eyes, waiting and watching as the man killed his engine, pushed open the door and emerged from his car in one easy movement.

He was tall. Very tall and dark. Her green eyes took him in with a quick stirring of surprise. He didn't look Scottish. His skin was olive and his hair was dark and thick, curling into the nape of his neck. Nothing about him looked local. From his physical appearance to the angular lines of his face that spoke of power, self-assurance and worldly-wise experience.

He looked like a city-dweller, she thought with a rush of disdain. The usual high-powered type she had spent years dealing with. A mover and a shaker who did deals and transformed the whole process of money-making into a number-one priority. She had spent many a long business lunch with types like this one, men in love with themselves and casually indifferent to anything that stood in the way of them getting what they wanted. In fact, she had made the irreparable mistake of actually doing more than just business with one of these types and look where that had got her.

It was only after an inordinately long time that she realised that the man was watching her watching him, his expression cool, calculating and utterly unruffled by her curiosity. Irritating, considering that he was on her property.

'Yes?' she asked, not moving, her hands still shading her face from the glare of the sun. 'May I help you?'

'Now, that's a big question,' the man drawled, slamming his car door and walking lazily towards her.

He was at least six feet three, Sara realised a little nervously. He towered over her in a way few men did. She was five-ten in bare feet and quite used to looking down on a great number of the men she had come into contact with over the years. There was also something a little scary about him. Was it the way he moved? Or his eyes? Deep blue, she could see now that he was closer, and strangely contained.

'Who are you and what do you want?' Sara demanded quickly, realising for the first time just how isolated this damned Rectory was.

Jumpy, James thought now that he had got over his astonishment at seeing the net-twitching spinster in the flesh. She was nothing like what he had expected. What the hell was a woman like this one doing out here? The mild curiosity he had experienced during the drive to the Rectory had crystallised into something pleasurably invigorating.

Jumpy and defensive. Why? Shouldn't she be flinging out the welcome mat and hustling to make tea for the friendly local visitor who had come to make her feel right at home and show her how warm her neighbours could be?

'So you're the new girl in town,' James drawled when he was finally standing in front of her. 'You picked the best month to move up here, I must say. June is usually kind. Lots of sun and blue skies.'

His blue eyes never left her face. Sara could feel his inspection and it was an uninvited intrusion into her space.

'You haven't told me your name,' she said flatly, edging slightly so that she was positioned in front of the kitchen door, making it quite clear that there was no automatic invitation to step inside.

'Nor have you told me yours. And I'm James Dalgleish.' He extended his hand and Sara found hers enclosed in long, strong fingers.

'Sara King.' She pulled her hand politely free and resisted the urge to massage it.

'Freddie's…niece perhaps?'

'That's right.'

'Funny, he never mentioned having any relatives,' James said thoughtfully, 'and I certainly don't recall any coming to visit.' He gave her a smile that didn't quite conceal the lazy challenge that seemed implicit in his comment.

Sara flushed and remained silently uncooperative. Did he, she wondered, think that she was some kind of opportunist? Would that be the general reaction of everyone in the town who had probably been discussing her furiously while she had holed herself up in her house and spent her time trying to work out why on earth she had come to this far-flung place?

'Mum!'

Her head whipped around at Simon's shout.

'My son,' she said, by way of explanation.

'You're married?'

'No.' She heard the scramble of footsteps heading towards the kitchen and gave a little sigh of irritation at her visitor, who continued to stand with implacable resolve by the door. 'Look, I'm rather busy at the moment.'

'I'm sure you are. Moving house is always a headache.' James watched as she raised one slender hand and pushed some flyaway red hair away from her face. 'You need to sit and relax. I'll make you a cup of coffee.'

'I—'

'Mum, I'm thirsty. Can you come and see my garage?'

'This is Simon,' Sara introduced reluctantly as her five-year-old son appeared next to her and proceeded to stare unblinkingly at their visitor. 'Simon, how many times have I told you that you should wear your slippers around the house?' By way of reply, he popped his thumb into his mouth and continued to inspect James curiously.

'Being barefoot is so much easier, isn't it?' James said, stooping down until he was on the same level as the boy.

What was the story here? he wondered. Having planned to call on this woman so that he could find out how serious she was about living in the Rectory and how much he would be prepared to give her to buy her out, had even planned on suggesting other parts of the town where she could live if she wanted, he now found himself holding back on stating the reason for his visit in preference to discovering more about the red-haired woman and her child.

'Um,' Simon agreed, still sucking on his thumb.

'So you've built a garage? Anything I would want to send my own cars to?'

'Do you have children, Mr Dalgleish?'

James glanced up at her. 'Child-free.'

Now, I wonder why I'm not surprised at that, Sara thought. Lord, but how long would it take for her to get over the bitterness that still burned the back of her throat at the thought of Simon's father?

'How about that cup of coffee?' He stood up with a questioning look and Sara felt a little shiver race along her spine. It was almost as though he could read her mind and was calmly determined to stay his ground in the face of her reluctance. And she had to stop being reluctant. She knew that. She would have to go into the town sooner rather than later, if only to buy provisions for herself and Simon, and she would have to meet her new neighbours. Hiding was not an option.

'Come in.' She smiled another tightly polite smile while he headed through the door with the familiarity of someone who knew the place.

As he would, she thought. In a place of this size, everyone would know everyone else. From the looks of him, he was probably the local professional. A banker or a lawyer of some sort who fancied himself a cut above the rest.

She poured juice for Simon, who hovered by the table and ignored his slippers, which were by the chair. His baggy, long shorts made his thin legs seem even thinner and she reminded herself that he was the reason she had moved up here.

'Now, shall I come and put on a video for you, Simes? Your favourite cartoon, perhaps?'

'Can you play with me?' he asked hopefully, and she shook her head with a grin.

'Nice try. I'm just going to have a quick cup of coffee with Mr Dalgleish and then maybe we can go out and do some gardening. I'll let you use the watering can.'

'The big one?'

'If you can handle it.'

'I have some soil.' Simon turned gravely to James. 'For planting vegetables.'

'Really?' He didn't know much about children but this boy was so serious and so *thin*. He looked as though one wisp of a Scottish breeze would blow him off his feet, never mind the harshness of winter. 'Any in particular?'

'Beans.'

'Would those be baked beans?' James grinned and for the first time Simon smiled, a wide smile that brought a light to his face.

'With sausages and chips,' he said, giggling.

Sara felt something uncomfortable tug inside her and she frowned at James. 'Come on, Simes. Let's go and see what video we can put on for you.' She held out her hand and curled her fingers around her son's little ones.

When she returned to the kitchen it was to find that coffee had been made and was waiting for her. James was sitting at the kitchen table, his body turned away from her as he looked out of the French doors, which were sprawled open on to the front garden that rolled down towards the lane at the bottom and open countryside beyond that.

It was funny, but the house had felt so damned hollow since she had moved in. Now his presence filled it, making her edgy and defensive and for the first time turning her thoughts away from herself and the enormity of the mistake she had made.

'There was no need for you to make the coffee.' Sara stepped through into the kitchen and he turned slowly in his chair until he was looking directly at her. Those eyes, she thought, a little confused. Midnight-blue and thickly fringed with black eyelashes. Seriously disconcerting eyes.

'No problem. It won't be the first time I've made coffee in this kitchen.'

'You knew my uncle.' She willed herself to get her legs together and moved towards the opposite end of the kitchen table, pouring herself some coffee from the percolator *en route*, and sat down, cradling the mug between both hands.

'Everyone knew Freddie.' He gave her a long, measured look. Feeling out the land, he thought. How long had it been since he had last done that with a woman? Or anyone, for that matter? 'He was something of a local character. As you might know...or do you?' He raised his cup to his lips, sipped some of the coffee and regarded her over the rim of the cup.

'Is that why you came here, Mr Dalgleish? To try and pry into my life and find out what I'm doing here?'

'The name is James. And of course that's why I came here.' That, amongst other things, though those can wait for the moment, James thought. 'So...what *are* you doing here?'

Blunt to the point of rude, Sara thought, but rude to the point of getting whatever answers he wanted, because he put her in a position from which to evade his questions would have seemed like unnecessary shiftiness. And if she was to make a go of things here, unlikely though that seemed at this moment in time, then she would probably be meeting him again. To kick off by creating a bad atmosphere was not going to help either her or Simon.

Still, something about the man addled her and made her want to skulk away behind her defences to a position of safety.

'I...' She raised her green eyes to look steadily at him.

'Well, I inherited this house. If you *must* know, I never knew Uncle Fred. He and my father had a bit of a falling-out years ago, before I was born, and they never really patched things up. Anyway, moving up here…well, I thought that it…that it would be a good idea,' she finished lamely.

'*A good idea?*'

Sara felt her hackles rise. His tone did a good job of implying that any such good idea could loosely be translated as stupidity.

'And where have you come from?' James asked without giving her time to expand. 'South somewhere?'

'Everywhere is south of here,' Sara informed him coldly.

'*Touché.* I was actually referring to London.'

'I *was* living in London, yes.'

'With a child?'

'People do.'

More puzzling by the minute, James thought, sipping some of the coffee, which had gone lukewarm. He allowed himself to savour the thought of unravelling Sara King, finding the chink that would give him the leverage he wanted that would enable him to persuade her to sell the Rectory to him. He would be fair, more than fair, he decided, but he would get what he wanted in the end. And, looking at her now with her red hair, that pale, flawless skin, those translucent green eyes that were doing their best to be guarded but could not help simmering with fire, he had a sudden, disconcerting feeling that he was going to enjoy his dealings with her.

Physically, she was far removed from the type of women he tended to be attracted to. She was too tall, too slender, too pale. But there was still something about her that carried the unexpected. Perhaps the hint of a sharp brain that did not conform to what was expected of it.

'Are you finished with your coffee?' Sara asked, rising to her feet, one hand already outstretched to take his cup. 'I hate to rush you away, but I really have a million things to do and Simon will start acting up in a minute if I don't go through.'

'Have you been to the town yet?' Of course she hadn't. She had managed to keep herself to herself. 'Met any of the locals?'

Sara was grateful to be able to look away from those penetrating eyes as she moved towards the kitchen sink with both their cups in her hands. 'Not yet, no.'

'Then I insist you come to a luncheon party my mother is having on Sunday.'

'I...'

'You might as well satisfy their curiosity,' he commented drily, 'or they will simply start fabricating half-truths about you. Why did you choose to live here if you are afraid of facing the people you will find yourself living amongst?'

'I'm not afraid of any such thing!'

'Twelve precisely. You can't miss the house. It's the one next to yours. First left.' He stood up and Sara followed him with her eyes as he walked towards the kitchen door, giving her a brief salute before disappearing outside towards his car.

CHAPTER TWO

'SO WHAT'S she like?'

'Red hair. Green eyes. Tall. Has a child, a boy.'

'No, James, I meant what is she *like*? You know. Chatty, sociable, boring, *what*?'

Good question, James thought. He looked down at Lucy Campbell and then absentmindedly out towards the direction of the Rectory. She hadn't shown up. It was now four in the afternoon, lunch had been served, a splendid buffet of cold meats and salads, which had been eaten on the sprawling back patio with its rich scent of flowers. Croquet had been played amateurishly by a handful of the guests. There had been some talk of lawn tennis, but this had fizzled out to nothing because most of the guests had had too much of the very fine white wine to drink and were disinclined to put themselves through the effort of running around trying to hit a tennis ball over a net.

'James?'

He focused on the woman in front of him. By any standards, she was a pretty girl. Petite, blonde-haired, blue-eyed, impeccably haute-coutured and with the regulation cut-glass voice. Unfortunately, she irritated the hell out of him, and she was irritating him now, gazing up at him with the expectant expression of someone looking forward to a bit of juicy gossip.

'She seems pleasant enough,' he expanded with a shrug. He sipped some of his wine and found his gaze straying again in the direction of the Rectory.

'Pleasant?'

'No obvious psychological problems that I could spot,' he said edgily. Just damned hostile, he thought to himself. Was that a reaction to *him* in particular, he wondered, or men in general? He had found himself thinking about her more than he had anticipated and the fact that he was thinking about her now annoyed him.

'Very droll, James.' Lucy smiled a coquettish little smile, a smile she had perfected over the years and one that usually had men melting. It didn't appear to be working now. 'That's one of the things I absolutely *adore* about you.'

'Sorry?'

'You were telling me all about your fascinating new neighbour.' She held on to the smile but with difficulty. 'So she's tall, has red hair and seems pleasant. Is that all? What about this son of hers? What do you think they're doing here? *Really?* Would you like to know what *we* think?'

James didn't have to ask her who the *we* were. He knew well enough. Her little clique of privileged friends, four of whom had trooped along with their parents to the luncheon.

'You can tell me if you feel inclined,' he said discouragingly.

'Well, *we* all think that she's a bit of a nobody who's suddenly found herself the owner of a pretty nice house, you must admit, and has decided to land herself up here on the off-chance of meeting some dashing man to pick up the bill for her and her child.' Lucy drained her glass of wine. Her eyes were sparkling, over-bright. She had had, James thought with distaste, too much to drink.

'Really.'

'So you'd better watch out.' The blue eyes hardened

even though the pink, half-opened mouth continued to smile invitingly. 'She'll be after you before you know it.'

'Oh, I shouldn't think so,' James drawled, but he had a sudden vision of her stripping off to reveal a slender, pale body. He imagined her high, pert breasts and that long hair hanging around her in a tousled mane. He shoved one hand in his trouser pocket and took another mouthful of wine. His last girlfriend had been small, voluptuous and dark-haired. A sexy little thing with a penchant for expensive presents and designer outfits. Very rewarding for a while until her conversation, or lack of it, had begun to make itself felt over and above her physical assets.

'Of course she will,' Lucy was saying, half in jest, half serious. 'She's probably eyed you up as a good catch and is plotting how she can net you. And you men are so gullible, you won't know what's coming until it's hit you like a freight train.'

'I think,' James lowered his head slightly, 'you must be talking about the men *you* sleep with, Lucy, because *I* certainly do not fit that particular description.' Just the opposite, he thought drily. He'd already had one collision with that particular type of freight train and he was in no danger of ever having another.

No wonder the woman had not been inclined to discover the charms of the locals. If she knew the rumours circulating about her, she would stay away for the rest of her natural life. Lucy and her friends might not be permanent residents of the place, choosing to work in Edinburgh and travel back home to their parents on the occasional weekend, but if they were discussing Sara King and her motives then he would bet his mansion on the fact that their parents were as well.

And he had to admit that the thought had crossed his own mind. Before he had met her.

If Lucy had been witness to his brief visit the day before then talk about motives and gold-digging and the search for a husband would not be figuring highly in her conversation, because Sara King had shown not the slightest interest in him as anything other than a nosy neighbour she wanted to get rid of as quickly as possible.

He wondered wryly if this wasn't the reason why he had been spending so much time thinking about her. The fact that he had so obviously failed to impress her when in fact wowing women had always been a talent he had taken utterly for granted.

His mother was calling him over, urging him to participate in a new game of croquet, with two teams competing for a bottle of champagne. It was simply too glorious a day for them to go inside, and croquet, she whispered into his ear with a smile, was a sedate enough game to accommodate old age and tipsiness.

'I'll play on one condition,' James said, *sotto voce*, 'and that's if I'm spared the company of Lucy Campbell. There's only so much of that girl's wittering a man can take.'

'I thought you liked her!' Maria said in surprise and her son gave her a look of dry disbelief. 'Or at least didn't mind her,' she amended.

'Reminds me too much of certain social climbers I meet in London,' he said dismissively. 'Young, rich and a little too much in love with themselves.' He placed one foot neatly on a mallet lying on the grass by him and flicked it up, catching it with one hand.

'In which case, it's a good thing I hadn't lined her up for you as a prospective wife,' Maria smiled.

'No need for you to line me up with anyone, Mama. According to our dear debutante Lucy,' he flicked his head in the general direction of the Rectory, 'someone is already lining herself up to fill the role.'

'Oh, yes?' Maria cocked her head to one side and looked interestedly at her son. 'And who might that be?'

'Don't pretend the innocent with me, Mama,' James said with a slow grin. 'This is the original nesting bed of the malicious rumour, and Lucy and her clique of friends have already begun circulating one.'

'Which is…?'

'That our new neighbour is a money-grabbing gold-digger on the look-out for a prospective husband.'

'You have met her. You do not agree, then?' Maria asked casually and James gave a snort of laughter. 'Perhaps they are right.' She stole a curious look at her son, who was staring grimly out towards the Rectory. He had invited the girl over and she had failed to appear. She, Maria, had made no comment on this, but she knew that her son had been unsurprisingly annoyed. It wasn't often that his orders, which they always were, however prettily he tried to package them, were ignored.

'Perhaps,' Maria mused speculatively, 'she *is* on the look-out for a nice, eligible, rich man…'

'In which case she's barking up the wrong tree. Anyway, I can spot an opportunist a mile off and I can't think of anyone less on the look-out,' he said, his head filling with the images of the dismissive look she had thrown at him when he had stepped out of his car and the impatient resignation with which she had greeted his offer to make her a cup of coffee. 'She struggled to invite me into the Rectory, for God's sake!'

'What a shame,' Maria murmured teasingly, 'and how did you cope with the shock of not being fawned upon by a woman?'

'Women do not fawn over me, Mama,' he denied vigorously, but he flushed at the accuracy of her dart. He was fully and cynically aware that he possessed just the right combination of attributes to make a woman's head turn. 'And this one certainly didn't.'

'So your plans to buy the Rectory have taken a nose-dive, am I right?'

'Oh, I wouldn't rush into assuming any such thing.' But he had no idea how he was going to persuade her to sell. She hadn't struck him as the sort of woman who could be talked into doing anything she didn't want to do.

'Well, if she does not like you, James, then she is hardly going to agree to selling something she has travelled hundreds of miles to possess.' Maria looked out to where several of the guests were already trying to decide who should be in what team. Constance Campbell, who usually shifted automatically into the role of organising everyone else, was having a hard time with guests who were tipsy enough to get a kick out of thwarting her.

But I could get to know her, couldn't I…? James reflected. Discover the chink in her armour. The Rectory was beautiful but frankly falling to bits. If he got to know her, well, he could just help her along the way to realising just how much needed doing to the place and how much easier it would be to shift the potential headache to someone else. Namely him. No good barging in when she still had her little head in the clouds, but a few carefully placed remarks might work wonders.

'Who knows?' he answered in a distracted voice. 'Anyway, shall we get on with this wretched game of croquet? You know I can't stand the sport.'

'I know.' She touched his cheek briefly and lovingly. 'Not vigorous enough for you. It is nice having you home here.'

'And it'll be even nicer when this lot depart. You know what they say about too much of a good thing.'

As it turned out, it was after six before the last of the guests left and after eight by the time a thoughtful James had eaten dinner, which was served informally in the breakfast room off the kitchen. His mother chatted inconsequentially about the luncheon party, amusing him with barbed remarks about village gossip and what was happening with whom and where. Normally, they would have retired to their favourite sitting area, the one which offered the most tantalising views. It would have provided a soothing and welcome end to a fairly hectic day, but James was in no mood to be soothed. His mother's voice drifted in calm waves over his head but he was thinking. Thinking about what she had said earlier, her throwaway remark that their Rectory neighbour might prove to be as stubborn as the uncle she had clearly never met.

The train of his thoughts made him edgy and he knitted his dark brows together in a frown, only realising his distraction when his mother said something which he was obliged to ask her to repeat.

'There is no need for the Rectory,' Maria sighed. 'Have I not told you this over and over? If the manor is converted to a hotel, I can simply live in a suite.'

'And share your dinner with the hotel guests?' He gave her a brooding frown that arrogantly denied his mother doing any such thing. 'Walk out into the garden so that you can join clusters of other people admiring the flowers? Have your evening drink brought to you by a waiter on his way to serve other people their evening drinks? I would rather,' he rasped, 'abort my ideas of converting this place than suffer you going through any of that.'

'Why do you think Miss King did not come to our little

lunch party?' Maria asked, to change the subject, and he shrugged.

'Perhaps the thought of socialising with us all filled her little soul with terror. Although,' he couldn't help but add, 'believe me, it would have been the other way around. *She* would have been the one filling *their* little souls with terror.'

'She made quite an impact on you, James, did she not?'

'I'll let you know tomorrow,' he said slowly, standing up and stretching. He raked his fingers through his hair and then turned to look at his mother.

'Why tomorrow?'

'Because I think I'll head across to Miss King and find out for myself why she did not appear when I specifically invited her.'

'You were piqued, weren't you?' Maria asked slyly.

'Hardly. It's simply that…I intend to buy her house and I won't be able to dangle money at the end of the carrot in an attempt to persuade her. Whatever brought her rushing up here, it wasn't poverty. From what I glimpsed of her possessions, at least the ones in the kitchen, she was not labouring under financial stress. So I shall simply have to dig deep into my reservoirs of persuasiveness to get what I want.'

'Does that not sound easy?' Maria murmured to herself, her dark eyes speculative.

'So I shall see you tomorrow, Mama.' He strolled to where she was sitting and kissed her once on each cheek, as he always had done ever since he was a boy, on his way back to boarding-school after the holidays, half longing to stay with his parents and enjoy his life in Scotland with the wide, open spaces around him, half longing to return to his friends with their boisterous camaraderie.

He was under no illusions as he later drove across to

the Rectory. Sara King wasn't going to welcome him in
with open arms. She hadn't the first time round, and she
was going to be even less enthusiastic this time. Especially
as it was after nine and he would probably have to drag
her out of bed with his banging on the kitchen door.
Neither prospect was sufficient to put him off the matter
at hand.

There were lights on, at least, when he pulled up outside
and he killed the engine of the car, sitting inside for a few
minutes before going out. Then he strode out, peered
through one of the kitchen windows at the side just in case
she was busying herself in there, and, not seeing her,
banged on the knocker.

From upstairs, where she had just finished settling
Simon, Sara heard the authoritative knock and immediately
felt her spine straighten in irritation. It had been a hell of
a day and seeing James Dalgleish was the last thing she
needed, because she was certain that it was him. She had
not gone to his wretched luncheon party and now he had
come to check and find out why.

She half debated whether she should just ignore the
banging on the door and then remembered the way he had
continued standing there the previous day, not prepared to
budge an inch until she had invited him in. He would just
keep banging if she didn't answer until eventually Simon
woke up.

There was no time to try and make herself remotely
presentable. Her hair was loose, having been washed only
an hour before, and it fell around her shoulders in untamed
ringlets, still half-damp. Instead of her usual jeans, she was
wearing a loose grey jersey skirt that fell almost to her
ankles and a clingy ribbed grey top that ended just above
the waistband of the skirt.

'All right!' she muttered irritably under her breath, hurrying down the stairs before he broke down the door in his attempts to be heard. 'Did it occur to you that I might have been sleeping?' she greeted him angrily as she pulled open the kitchen door.

Idiot that she was, she had forgotten how overpowering he was. She had so successfully managed to shove him into the same category as her ex-boyfriend and her son's father, the mere thought of whom was enough to fill her throat with sour bile, that to see James standing there against the backdrop of the sinking sun almost made the breath catch in her throat.

He was so awesomely good-looking. He possessed skin that reacted warmly to the sun, and even in the space of a mere day he seemed browner than she recalled. The top two buttons of his cream shirt were undone, exposing the same, magnificently coloured skin, and the sleeves were roughly rolled back, and as her eyes dropped she took in his lean, muscled arms, then she blinked and her head cleared.

'No.'

'It's after nine at night!' she snapped, a little annoyed with herself for being bowled over, if only for a few seconds, by his physical allure.

'And you normally go to bed at nine?'

'Why are you here, anyway?'

'I've now been here twice and both times you've given me a pretty hostile reception. Tell me, is it just me or is it the entire human race?' He looked at her with lazy speculation in his eyes, knowing that she was taken aback by his comment, and while she was still struggling to come up with an appropriate response he continued in the same musing voice, 'I think it's the human race. Hence your willingness to bury yourself here without even bothering to take the time out to meet the people in whose community you have chosen to bury yourself.'

'And I think that you should keep your opinions to yourself considering I haven't asked you to share them with me.'

'Where is your little boy?'

'Asleep.'

'My mother was disappointed that you didn't come. She was looking forward to meeting you.'

Sara flushed guiltily. She'd had no compunction about letting *him* down, but she hadn't considered that she might be letting anyone else down in the process.

James could read it all from her expression and from the delicate bloom of colour that crept into her cheeks.

'She wondered,' he carried on, elaborating on this piece of fiction without the slightest twinge of guilt, 'whether you had perhaps been taken ill. The Rectory is quite isolated and, as far as she knows, your telephone might well not have been connected as yet.'

'I...yes, the telephone is connected. With Simon...'

'Of course. Still...she was concerned.'

There was a short, awkward pause during which James wondered whether he had piled it on too thick. But if she was going to develop a habit of slamming doors in his face, then he certainly could not afford to develop a habit of allowing it. Not if he wanted to get the Rectory. And anyway, he was, by nature, incapable of allowing anyone to slam a door in his face.

'Look...I apologise for not coming to your party... but...'

'It's a little chilly out here. That's the thing with summers in Scotland. However fine the day is, the night always reminds you not to take the warmth for granted. I merely stopped by to make sure that you were all right.' He half turned, curious to see whether the flush of guilt would be sufficient for her to stop him and it was. She invited him in. Not in the most gracious of voices and certainly with no noticeable enthusiasm, but it was an invitation he discovered he had been quite looking forward to and was all too keen to grasp.

'Tea?' she asked, once they were in the kitchen. 'Coffee? Something stronger?'

'Coffee would be fine.'

'I apologise for not coming to your mother's little party,' Sara repeated, spooning coffee into cups, with her back to him, 'but I couldn't. How was it? Did it go all right?'

'Couldn't...?'

Sara didn't answer. She poured boiling water into the cups, and a dash of milk straight from the long-life carton in the fridge. The fresh milk she had casually tossed into the cardboard box for the trip up had expired. The dreaded trip to the shops could no longer be avoided, that much was true. Nor could she allow her negative feelings about the place to influence her response to the people who lived there. If she did, then her life would be even more of a nightmare than it already was.

'Simon wasn't very well, I'm afraid,' she said brusquely, putting his cup down in front of him and taking the chair on the opposite side of the table from which she could observe him without that aura of his pervading her senses.

'What was wrong?' Under the merciless glare of the overhead light, he could see what he hadn't noticed before. Her face was drawn and there were anxious shadows under her eyes.

'He...suffers from recurrent chest infections. He's still got one now and he was a bit poorly today.' She swallowed a mouthful of coffee and shifted her eyes away from the blue ones studying her face.

'Is he all right now? I know Tom Jenkins, the local doctor. I could call him and get him out here to have a look.'

'Thank you, but no. Simon's a bit better now. He's upstairs sleeping. Anyway, I couldn't come to your mother's party because at twelve today I was busy dealing with his wheezing and coughing.'

'You should have driven over. Got me.' Why had he just said that? he wondered.

'Thanks, but I can deal with Simon on my own. I don't need any knights in shining armour to help me out. I've done it for the past five years and I'll carry on doing it.'

'I wasn't offering myself as a knight in shining armour.' James's voice was a shade cooler. 'I was merely suggesting that at this point in time I happen to be the only person you know in this town and as such, if you had needed help, it would have made sense to have come to me.'

'I told you, I didn't need any help. Look, if you don't mind, I haven't had anything to eat this evening. I'm going to make myself a sandwich. I'm sure you have much better things to do than hang around here watching me eat my dinner.'

'Sit down.'

'What?' Sara flashed him a smile of cool incredulity at the rasping command in his voice. 'For a minute there, I thought I heard you tell me to sit down.'

'Which just goes to show how accurate your hearing is.' Before she could stand up, which he knew she was going to do, he stood up himself and moved swiftly to where she was sitting, leaning over her with one hand splayed on the arm of her pine chair and the other on the table.

'What do you think you're doing?' Sara demanded in a high-pitched, unsteady voice.

'I am making sure you do as I say. Sit down and I'll make the sandwich for you. Tell me what you want in it and point me in the direction of the bread.'

'I...'

'You look exhausted. You've obviously been through one helluva long day. Now do as I say.'

'Or else what?' Sara flung at him. Their eyes clashed and she was mortified to find that she couldn't seem to stop looking at him. Up close, she could smell the fresh, clean scent of him, mingled with the erotic tang of sheer masculinity. It filled her nostrils until she felt as if she was going to faint. Instead, she blinked and clung on rapaciously to her pride. She didn't need this. She didn't need some man, a perfect stranger, to waltz into her house and try and give her orders, even if those orders were issued for her own benefit. She had had to fend for herself from a young age and she had carried on having to do it right the way through pregnancy, childbirth and motherhood.

'Oh, all right,' she snapped, just to get him to move away from her.

'Good.' James pushed himself up but continued to look down at her. 'Now, where's the bread?' he repeated.

'Bread bin on the dresser.' The dresser had been Freddie's. Sara herself had not possessed any such thing when she had lived in London. The kitchen in her flat had been all chrome, granite and smooth cherry wood. An old pine dresser would have been ludicrously inappropriate, but she had since discovered that it was an extremely useful item of furniture. She had kept Freddie's mismatched crockery in place, stashing her own out of sight, and there was a growing pile of Simon's things on the surface, stray colours, bits of Lego, various action-hero dolls in strangely contorted positions.

'This bread's mouldy,' James said, holding up the plastic bag.

He looked so ridiculous that she had to stifle a smile that crept up from somewhere and threatened to chisel away at her defences.

'Do you *know* how to make a sandwich?' she asked curiously. 'Have you *ever* made a sandwich in your life before?' He just didn't look the sandwich-making type.

'I happen to be a very good cook, actually. You haven't eaten any of this today, have you? Is there another loaf somewhere? No? Then I'll just have to make do, and before you start protesting, my original order to sit down still applies.' He tossed the bread in the bin and did a swift inventory of the modest kitchen, noting the uneasy mingling of her own things amongst Freddie's.

'You really don't have to,' Sara said automatically, but lord, it felt good to take the weight off her feet and have someone else do something for her for a change. She rubbed her hand across her eyes and stretched out her long legs.

'Tell me about London,' James said, pulling out a chopping board and then gathering what vegetables he could muster from the basket by the dresser. Everything, he noticed with interest, was as Freddie had left it. Either she had possessed surprisingly little herself or else could not be bothered to install her own things. Which said what? he wondered. 'What did you do there?'

'Where did you learn to cook?'

James glanced over to her. She had rested her head back against the chair and her eyes were closed, as if she was simply too weary to keep them open, and for the first time since he'd arrived he felt a pang of guilt at having foisted his company onto her at nine in the evening. Then he reminded himself that she would have had to eat anyway, and she had actually done quite well from him considering he was here cooking up a pasta dish for her, not an activity he was known to do for any woman.

'At the hands of my mother during the school holidays,' James informed her, allowing her change of topic to ride. For the moment. 'She's Italian and prides herself on her culinary skills. As soon as I could hold a sharp knife, I was given things to chop.' His eyes flitted over to find that she was staring at him, and for no logical reason, because he was vastly accustomed to being on the receiving end of women's stares, he felt himself stiffen in response. 'And as soon as I was tall enough, I was taught how to use the Aga.'

'Your mother was a chef?'

'My mother was a model from Naples who met my father in London. Much to her agency's disgust, he charmed her into marrying him after a shockingly brief whirlwind romance and removed her to the back of nowhere, where she flourished. She relished breezing into the lives of all the locals, who had never met a real Italian before and had certainly never had one live in their midst. She held huge parties in winter and taught the wives how to cook homemade pasta. After a couple of years they were eating out of her hand.'

Sara listened to the smile in his voice and felt her heart contract. Whatever else she thought of him as a man, and cooking her a meal would do nothing to alter her opinions, he loved his mother deeply and that counted for a lot.

'Hence,' he told her, 'my cooking skills.'

'And I always thought that it was the other way around,' Sara said, 'the woman stuck at home cooking the food while the man just did whatever he damn well pleased.'

'Has that been your experience?' James asked casually, sliding his eyes over to her and taking in the way her body language altered and her face became watchful and closed.

The thought of drawing out whatever story she had to tell, finding out what the hell made her tick, coursed through his veins in a sudden, exhilarating rush. It was a sensation so alien to him that he belatedly reminded himself of the Rectory, which was, after all, the prize to be won.

'I never asked you whether you were married,' Sara said, surprised to find that she had automatically assumed that he wasn't when she should have assumed just the opposite. 'Would your wife be happy about your cooking food for me?' she continued slowly, trying to picture the sort of woman he would be married to. Beautiful, blonde and brainless, presumably. She had learnt over the years the better-looking and more powerful the man, the less they wanted a wife who could compete with them. Not restful enough.

'You insult me,' James said coldly. 'If I were married, I wouldn't be here. I would be with my woman.'

The way he said that, the casual male acceptance of possessing a woman the way he might possess a piece of furniture, should have had every liberated bone in her body rushing to form a picket line, but instead she felt a searing heat rip through her.

'Cooking for her?' Sara asked lightly, to stop herself from analysing her reaction which didn't make sense.

'Not necessarily,' he said with lazy amusement. 'I might find other things to do in a kitchen that don't necessarily involve food.'

Sara's stomach curled warmly at the blatant image he had casually tossed at her. 'Well,' she tried to gather her scattered wits and speak in a normal voice, 'at any rate, whatever you're cooking smells very good.'

'And it will taste even better,' he assured her, spooning pasta onto a plate and pouring sauce over it straight from the saucepan. It was a rich sauce which he had concocted using a handful of ingredients which hadn't appeared to be dead or in the process of dying, like the three tomatoes he had uncovered next to the onions.

He placed the plate in front of her. 'Now eat.'

'You like giving orders, don't you?' But her mouth was watering and she dived into the food with enthusiasm, not realising how hungry she had been until she saw the bottom of the plate.

'I prefer to see them as instructions.'

'And do you give instructions to all the locals?' she asked, scraping some of the fabulous tomato sauce onto her spoon and relishing it.

'To the locals? Why would I do that?'

'Because you live here?'

'I have a house here and my mother lives here.'

Sara looked at him over the rim of her spoon. 'And where do you live?'

'In London.'

'Ah. That makes sense.'

The shutters were back up, he saw. She carefully closed her fork and spoon and took her plate to the sink, offering him the unrevealing view of her back as she washed the crockery and placed it on the draining board next to her.

'And why does that *make sense*?'

She turned around and perched against the sink, supporting herself with her hands on either side of her, her fingers curled over the edge of the counter.

'I thought you were a little too urbane for around here,' she said. 'A little too sophisticated.'

'Should I take that as a compliment?'

'You can take it any way you want to, although it wasn't meant as one.'

'I presume you have something against urbane, sophisticated men?' James stood up and shoved his hands into his pockets. 'Has that got anything to do with Simon's father, by any chance?'

The silence stretched tautly between them until Sara forced herself to smile with tight politeness at him. After all, he *had* cooked her a meal.

'Thank you so much for cooking for me. It was delicious.'

'Most sincerely spoken.' James walked slowly towards her and the closer he got, the tenser she became, until he was standing inches away from her. Then he reached out and caged her in with his hands, leaning towards her so that their faces were only inches apart. 'But you haven't answered my question.'

'And I don't need to!' she flared angrily. 'My life is none of your business. I'm a very private person and I intend to stay that way.'

'Then, lady, you came to the wrong place. Because I, for one, intend to get right down to the bottom of you.'

He stood back and walked towards the kitchen door. 'We'll meet again.' And he meant every word of it. Without even realising it, she challenged him, and he had never been able to resist a challenge.

CHAPTER THREE

THERE was no need to drive to the nearest sizeable town for her shopping, even though she was sorely tempted to do just that, if only so that she could savour the anonymity which she now found that she perversely craved.

Nestled cosily against the vast backdrop of mountains was the local village. Sara, with one eye on the map next to her and the other on the twisty road, rounded a bend straight into suburbia.

From his car seat in the back, Simon was peering through the window in apparent fascination at the scenery. So fascinated, in fact, that his mouth was parted to accommodate a thumb he had forgotten to suck.

And yes, she had to admit that the scenery was spectacular. From the Rectory to the small town, there were times when the winding road almost seemed to be an insolent intrusion into Mother Nature. Every so often, a sudden bend in the road would offer a tantalising glimpse of flat, glassy water in the distance. She had no idea whether this was an estuary or a loch but, whatever it was, Simon had been enthralled. She, slightly less so. The more magnificent the landscape, the more she longed for the concrete jungle in which she had spent all of her twenty-six years. Noise pollution, air pollution and having to make do with window-boxes in place of a garden had never seemed more enticing.

'Houses!'

'At last,' Sara muttered. They had passed a few big old houses on the journey but these were real houses with real roads that did real things, like branch out in various directions. 'I was beginning to think that we had been transported into the Twilight Zone.'

'What's the Twilight Zone?'

'Should we just drive straight through here until we get to a proper town,' Sara mused aloud, 'or face it?'

'I'm thirsty.'

'Then I guess we'll face it.'

The local village turned out to be bigger than she had expected. Not quite the cluster of basic shops, leaning shoulder-to-shoulder against one another so that the owners could while away their time gossiping outside. The flat white fronts and grey stone façades of the houses, which sprang out from the main street, eventually gave way to small shops offering everything from fly-fishing equipment to guided tours. Further along Sara came to the central square, dominated by a statue of whose identity she had no idea, although his warrior-like bearing didn't suggest the local poet. Cars were neatly parked in slots in front of the monument and spreading around the square was a further assortment of shops, bigger and less picturesque than their counterparts further down the road.

She pulled into a parking space, manoeuvering her small black car until it was resting snugly between a four-wheel-drive on one side and weathered pick-up truck on the other.

'Right,' she said, fetching Simon out of the car and looking around her with some interest. 'We can get lost here.'

'Why would we want to get lost?' he asked in a bewildered voice, and she squeezed his hand gently.

'It's just a saying. Now, where first? Supermarket? Quaint craft shop with hand-knitted jumpers? Pharmacy to check out the medicines for you just in case you get another chest infection. Or maybe just an ice cream before we start doing anything at all?'

This wasn't going to be as bad as she had feared, Sara thought as they headed for the nearest tea shop. She wouldn't quite be able to lose herself here, but at least she wouldn't be singled out as the intruder who had gone to live at the Rectory. Perhaps, she told herself, she could see this as a sort of short holiday. Stay until the middle of August, perhaps, admit the mistake she had made and then head back down south with her tail between her legs. They wouldn't have to return to London. They could live somewhere just outside, somewhere as peaceful as this place without being quite as scarily remote.

She was so busy turning her thoughts over in her head that she failed to notice the significant hush that greeted her breezy entrance into the shop.

She focused and then saw what she had missed when she had first entered, with Simon jabbering away about what flavour ice cream he wanted while she frowningly chewed over thoughts of flight in her head.

All heads were turned in their direction. A table of six elderly women seemed particularly interested. Even the ruddy-cheeked, fresh-faced girl behind the counter had stopped what she had been doing to stare.

Sara ventured a weak smile, her eyes skittering away from the gang of six sitting by the window with their cups of tea and little delicate plates of scones and cream.

'A table?' she asked in a lame voice. 'For two?' She could hardly believe that she was the same assertive woman who had once been a powerful career woman.

'You must be the new girl at the Rectory!' The booming voice stopped her in her tracks and forced her to look across at the six women. 'We've all been dying to meet you! Have we not, ladies?'

'Come, my dear, and let us have a proper look at you and your delightful little boy!'

Sara helplessly looked at the girl behind the old-fashioned wooden counter, who shot her a sympathetic smile.

'I…I…' she stammered, making her way to the table.

'Naturally we were curious about this relative of Freddie's. The old rogue never breathed a word about having a niece. Did he, ladies?'

'You poor thing. Could you not get away from that big old place a little sooner? Heaven knows, you must have been up to your elbows in it! And you with a wee lad as well to look after.'

'Would that be why we haven't spied you in town before?'

'I…I…' Sara repeated weakly.

'And what's *your* name, child? I bet you've come here for an ice cream. This place makes the best ice creams in Scotland!'

'And you should know, Angela. You eat far too many of them for your own good.'

'Now, dear, why don't you pull up a chair and we can all have a cosy little chat.'

'I…well…' Sara licked her lips nervously, while Simon hesitantly accepted a teacake from one of the ladies and began chatting in his low, childish voice to her.

'You might be able to help us! We're trying to sort out the summer fête at the manor. Some fresh input might be just what is needed, would you not agree, ladies? And no, Valerie, we are *not* going to be accommodating your daughter's suggestion about a disco. For a start, Maria would go mad!'

'Well, well, well…' a familiar velvety voice drawled from behind her and Sara felt as though fingers had lightly slithered up her spine, making her pulses race. 'I see you've been caught by the local witches.' There was a wicked grin in his voice when he said that, and Sara didn't need to turn around to imagine the expression on his face. One of utter charm. She could see it in the way the six ladies tittered. 'Be warned, you may not escape this place in one piece.'

'Now, now, young man!'

'Where's your mother, James? She said she would be here by eleven. I'm very much afraid she's missed the first pot of tea.'

'Trouble with one of the gardeners. His daughter's been admitted into hospital, it would seem.'

'That would be young Emma. Baby's on its way, poor thing.'

One of the gardeners? Sara wondered whether she had heard wrong. She had gleaned that the man lived in a big house and was doubtless wealthy or else how could he have a place in London as well, but *how big was his house if he needed more than one gardener to control the lawn*?

Suddenly she didn't want to be here, didn't want to feel his breath against her averted face, because he was standing so close to her that she could. Nor did she want to find herself wondering about him. She already knew enough.

'I... If you don't mind, I have a thousand things to do before I go home, and…and…'

'You've frightened her,' he said on a low laugh, and Sara had the impression that in some peculiar way he was toying with her.

'Don't be ridiculous!' she snapped, whipping around to look at him. Her blazing eyes made little impact. He continued to smile in amusement and had not even been surprised into stepping back. She felt engulfed by his physical presence and hurriedly spun back round so that she was looking at the women, although she knew that her cheeks were burning.

'I really don't mean to be rude, but…but Simon, my son, is just getting over a chest infection and I wanted to try and make it to the pharmacy to buy a few things for him.'

'A chest infection? Oh, you poor wee thing.'

Looking down, Sara wryly observed how he puffed himself out in the face of all the sympathetic tittering from the old ladies.

'Is that one of the reasons that you came up here?' one of the ladies asked. 'They often say that clean air is good for respiratory conditions and we know you lived in London. Is that not a fact, Mary? Didn't your Eleanor have to leave London because her asthma began to get worse?'

'Well, as a matter of fact,' Sara mumbled, keenly aware of the man standing behind her and not really sure why allowing him access to this little sliver of personal information was so off-putting, 'it was one of the reasons.'

'Well, of course we must let you get on. Sandra, dear! Another pot of tea. I can see Maria on her way. If she can manage to get away from that old fool Jenkins. Now, my dear, I hope we'll be seeing a lot more of you!'

'And I'm sure,' James said, 'that the feeling is entirely reciprocated, isn't it? Sara?' His voice was like dark chocolate curling around her name and something hot and alive deep inside her kicked, unbidden, into life. It was something she didn't want to feel and she responded accordingly by pushing it away.

'Of course.' She managed a polite smile, eager to go now that she had established her excuse.

'Oh, good, because there's our little summer dance at the village hall…'

'You're more than welcome to help decorate…'

'On Friday evening. Barbecue if the weather permits...'

'And it will. If those weathermen are anything to go by, not that they usually are...'

'Friday,' Sara said lamely. 'I'd love to, but Simon—'

'I'm sure my mother would be more than happy to babysit,' James interjected, knowing full well where her protest was leading. He hadn't planned on staying quite as long as Friday, but the minute he had removed the objection from her mouth he was filled with an inexplicable urge to prolong his sojourn.

Get to know her, he argued to himself with every semblance of rationality. How else does one win ground unless one is fully aware of the layout?

And, irritating though the admission was, he still knew practically nothing about her and he wanted to find out more. It was a first for him. Hidden depths were not something that he particularly looked for, or for that matter had ever found, in any of the women he had dated. And he liked it that way. That way there was no room for nasty surprises.

'I couldn't possibly...' There was a hunted look in her eyes which he blithely ignored.

'You would be doing her a great favour. She adores children and would love nothing better than to spend the evening with Simon.'

'Well, Simon is very shy with—'

'You could even bring him up to our house. There's a room occupied solely by the most elaborate train set a child could ever hope to find...'

'Train set?' Simon's ears had pricked up, and with a sigh of frustrated resignation Sara conceded defeat.

'So...' he had followed her out of the café, out into the glare of the sun '...you came here because of Simon...why did you wait five years? Surely he would have been suffering from recurrent chest infections from birth?'

'Have you nothing better to do than tag along behind me?'

'Not at this point in time,' he informed her, proving, she thought, that he was every bit as thick-skinned as she had deduced from their first meeting.

Indeed, at this point in time, the business he had intended to do while his mother spent a pleasant couple of hours with her cronies had faded into the background. Right now, he could think of nothing better than glancing over to catch sight of that vibrant red hair that was today caught up in a tortoiseshell clip that barely contained its luxuriant waywardness, that creamy white skin, tinged pink at her discomfort at having to endure his presence.

'You never bought your ice cream,' he pointed out suddenly. 'I suppose our resident crew called you across before you could get to put in your order.' Everyone was curious, he reasoned, and so she would not be able to resist letting her natural curiosity have a wander, even though the determined tilt of her head told him that she would have liked nothing better.

'Who *are* they?' Sara asked, glancing into the windows of some of the shops they were strolling past, catching the occasional look in her direction and uncertain whether this was due to her or to curiosity about why the man at her side was with her.

'Supermarket?' he asked, leaving aside her question for the moment.

She wouldn't have immediately guessed. 'With travel brochures in its window?'

'That's Bill MacKenzie next door. Pays for some of the window space and Trevor never could resist a buck.'

The quaintness of the arrangement brought a smile to

her lips, a smile that he noticed, just as he noticed the reluctance behind it, as though it was dragged out of her.

'Look, why don't you go and get your shopping and I'll take Simon for that ice cream? We can meet you in the square in half an hour.'

'No!'

The vehemence of her response surprised him and he looked at her levelly, his eyebrows raised.

'What's the problem?' he murmured.

'There's no problem. I just don't want to accept your offer. Isn't that enough for you? I have a lot of things to do before I head back home and Simon…needs to be with me.'

And I won't allow my son to get close to a man who sees me as a little mystery he'd like to have fun trying to solve while he's killing a few days here.

Every protective bone in her body had reared up into action at the thought of that. Simon had had enough disappointments in his short life what with having to deal with a father who was not particularly interested in him, who had routinely made arrangements to take him somewhere only to break them at the very last minute because something more important had come up.

In the space of a few still seconds, the past five years unreeled themselves in her head like a series of cinematic clips which had been edited and fast-forwarded to encapsulate her ex-partner and the misery he had brought to her life.

The pregnancy, Simon, Phillip's lack of support because, as he had ruefully informed her, he wasn't the marrying kind, still less the paternal sort. He had seen Simon occasionally but his life had been moving onwards and upwards. There was no time to fit in a sickly son who was too thin, too small and got ill all the time.

The only thing that had ever mattered to Phillip, if only she had been able to see that from the word go, was his career and the ambition to get even further with it. And here was James Dalgleish, who seemed to be as ambitious and career-oriented as Phillip, pretending to take an interest in her son, an interest that was never going to get anywhere, but try telling that to a vulnerable five-year-old child without a father.

She could easily cope with the likes of James Dalgleish. She was immune to men like him. But ice cream in the village square with her son? Oh, no, she thought, *I don't think so.*

'What's the matter?' James's voice seemed to come from a long way away and the sharpness of it snapped her out of her memories. She blinked and focused on him. 'For a minute there you looked as though you were about to pass out.'

'Did I?' Sara asked coldly.

Her tight, closed expression mirrored the iciness of her voice. Whatever she wanted most right at this very moment, and he would bet on this, was for him to disappear. But he wasn't going to do her that favour.

'Now, why would that be, I wonder?'

Sara licked her lips nervously. Her body seemed to have broken out in a fine film of clammy perspiration and she didn't like the way he was looking at her, with that sort of curious interest that made her feel a bit like a specimen being observed by a very clever, very dangerous scientist.

She also didn't care for what he was doing to her body, because even though her brain was furiously seeing with perfect clarity all the danger signs that were going off like alarm bells in her head, her body was behaving with a life of its own. Her breasts felt as though they were pulsing and there was a treacherous warmth spreading through her that illogically made her even angrier with the man standing unperturbed in front of her, looking at her as though he could read every little strand of thought in her mind. And if he couldn't, then he intended to probe until he could.

'What's Simon's relationship with his father?'

Colour drained from her face. *How dared he?*

'That's no business of yours!'

'Is it a secret?' He had asked the wrong question, he could see that now. Somehow he had managed to dig into a wound that was still raw, but hell, he would go for broke now. 'What's *your* relationship with him?' he asked.

Sara reacted on impulse. There was no longer any Simon by her side, no shops around her, no pavements teeming with people all out doing their shopping in the fine weather. There was just him.

Her open palm stung as it made fierce contact with his face and the sound of flesh hitting flesh shocked her almost as much as it shocked him, but before she could turn and flee the unpleasant scene she felt his fingers circle her wrist and he was bending over her, his mouth thinned into a flat, angry line.

'Don't,' he said with silky menace, 'ever do that again.'

'Or else what?' Sara demanded through gritted teeth. 'What will you do to me? Throw me in prison? Chain me to a post in the village square?'

'Such antiquated ideas,' James said with soft intent. 'Punishment comes in many different packages.' He lowered his head and his mouth made contact with hers, driving her back slightly, and in that moment of unsteady surprise his tongue found a way to plunder her mouth. It was a hard, savage kiss that ended almost before it began and he couldn't have thought of a more brutally effective punishment because Sara could only stare at him in silent shock.

Her lips felt bruised but it was inside that was really doing a wild, terrifying roller-coaster ride. She couldn't have been more affected if an electric current had been driven into her. Her whole body ached and throbbed and wanted in a way that filled her with fright and dismay.

'And don't forget,' he reminded her in a perfectly level voice, 'that my mother will be babysitting for you on Friday.' His deeply sensual mouth parted into a humourless smile. 'And don't, likewise, imagine that you can wriggle out of it. It's a small town and tongues wag. If you want to be happy here with your son, then I am sure you see the necessity of kicking off to the right start.'

His accuracy of the size of the town and the wagging of tongues struck home later that evening when, over dinner, his mother carefully closed her knife and fork and gave him one of those shrewd looks that he knew from experience promised a serious conversation.

'I knew that you had met our new neighbour,' Maria Dalgleish said ruminatively, 'but I had no idea that you had become quite so intimate with her.'

'Now, how did I know that that was coming?' James tossed his white linen napkin next to his plate and sat back in the chair, pushing it away from the exquisitely polished table so that he could cross his legs.

'A passionate kiss in the middle of town, James?' Her eyes flashed with sudden amusement and she looked down at the tips of her fingers. 'Surely you must have known that such a thing would have had...' she searched to find the appropriate phrase in English '...fall-out.'

James's eyes were brooding and uncooperative. He had known full well what the so-called fall-out of his actions would be, had known it even as he had lowered his head towards her. The possibility of *him*, the most prominent man in the area, probably in the whole of Scotland for that matter, going unnoticed was zilch.

But he had been compelled to. He had looked into those fiery green eyes, looked lower to the angrily parted lips, perfectly defined petal-pink lips, and he had been unable to resist tasting them. Only the knowledge that they were in public and her son was staring up at them wide-eyed and curiously accepting, had made him pull back from her. Or he would have carried on kissing her and he had wanted more. Much more. Just thinking about it now made his body react in a pleasurable but utterly inappropriate way.

'Because there are too many idle women in this place,' he said irritably, 'with nothing better to do than talk about other people.'

'So,' Maria said briskly, 'is it tomorrow that you are off? Or Wednesday? I had planned a meeting with the girls for tomorrow to discuss this summer fête at the manor, but of course I can easily cancel that and we can maybe go somewhere for lunch.'

'No need.' He sat frowning and thinking, cursing himself for having given in to his ridiculous male impulse to kiss the damned woman and expose her unwittingly to gossip. 'I've decided to stay until at least the weekend.' He refocused on his mother and added drily, 'I at least have some duty to escort Sara King to the local ball, having sullied her image in the first place.' He imagined her standing hesitantly on her own by the door of the village hall, having been forced to attend an event she clearly had not wanted to, while everyone stopped what they had been doing to look covertly at her. 'Which reminds me, I told her that you'll babysit her son, Simon. I hope you don't mind.'

'Mind? I will enjoy every minute of it. You know how much I love children.'

'And don't even think it, Mama,' James said wryly, toying with the slender stem of his wine glass, watching the remnants of his white wine swirl around. 'I'm not about to get involved with her. She's as elusive as a shadow and you know I have only ever been attracted to the straightforward type.' But even as the words had been uttered, he had a compelling vision of a tall, slender creature, with creamy white skin, breasts pushing forward like ripe fruit to be tasted. He drained his wine and stood up, ready to take his leave.

And Maria Dalgleish was more than happy to let him. She couldn't think while he hovered there, and thinking was what she felt like doing tonight.

'I shall show him your father's train set, shall I?' she asked with a smile and he nodded with a little shrug.

'Why not? He's bound to love it. I did.' Now that he had decided not to leave, just yet, he had business to see to. Thank God for computers, faxes, e-mails and all the technology that would enable him to run his empire away from his offices, if only for a while.

He would stay at home, he thought, and work. His visits to the estate were so short that no one would question the fact that he was no longer around in the town and he would not risk bumping into Sara again.

He had frightened her with his questions, appeared to have utterly panicked her with his ill-thought-out kiss. He would give her time to recover and build up her defences.

But the mere thought of those defences going up was enough to fire him up at the thought of breaking them down.

But go back up they would. Less than a mile away, Sara was feverishly thinking the same thing. She had spent the day in a state of charged confusion. Done her shopping and hurried back to the Rectory with Simon. Normally, being with him was always enough to take her mind off her problems, but today her mind was caught in a trap elsewhere, filled with images of James Dalgleish and the kiss he had forced upon her as fair retribution for her having slapped his face.

He would never have had his face slapped by a woman in his life before, she thought as she sat in the cosy snug with the television providing muted sound in the background. That arrogant, devastatingly attractive face would not have inspired anger in any woman he might have been out with. It would have inspired *craving* because everything about him, from the way he looked to the way he moved, was sexually mesmerising.

He had touched her and her body had shot up in flames, hot flames that licked every part of her. It would almost have been better if she could have put her response down to the needs of a woman who had been celibate for the past five years.

And they would be talking about her in the town. Their kiss hadn't exactly been conducted in the privacy of four walls.

But there were still some things that needed doing. Someone to come and install an extra phone line for her so that she could use the internet on her computer. Someone to come and link up her computer for goodness' sake, get it up and running. She had never had to bother with the nuts and bolts of the thing, but then in London she had had a secretary to do all that for her, to get the appropriate software technicians in when it was playing up. Even if she only intended to stay put for a limited period of time, she would still have to buy a book on computers, at least so that she could learn some of the rudiments herself.

After all the effort she had made to get here, though, the thought of running back down south now seemed exhausting. More change for Simon. And if she returned south, then how long before the headhunters began? Life was frantic down there.

She shook her head wearily and decided that she had better check out schools, get Simon registered, just in case.

That, too, would need a visit to the town. Balking at the prospect of meeting yet another set of people who knew her business was not going to do her any good.

But, as it turned out, her trip in on the Thursday was less of an ordeal than she had imagined. And she found out, really without asking, that James had left to return to London. This piece of information came from a girl in her twenties whose young boy ended up playing with Simon in a little park on the edge of the town where Sara had taken him to see some ducks. She herself had ended up sitting on the bench with the girl, to discover that her mother was one of the dreaded six and that she, Fiona, was the local vet's assistant.

'You won't be over-popular with some of our girls who think that James Dalgleish is up for grabs,' Sara was told with a laugh, 'but you'll be very popular with the rest of us who find that little lot extremely annoying. *That kiss* has been the most exciting thing to have happened here in months!'

That kiss was not going to happen again, at any rate, Sara thought on the Friday as she nervously contemplated going to the village hall, an invitation which had been thrust upon her and one which she was morally obliged to meet.

Fiona, at least, would be there, she consoled herself. She would have an ally should she need one. And James Dalgleish was safely tucked hundreds of miles away.

On her last trip to the town he had been nowhere in sight, and his absence made sense. Powerful businessmen like him were incapable of staying away from their offices for too long. It would almost be easier for their bodies to defy gravity than it would for their minds to defy the pull of the top-level business meeting.

She got dressed, and by seven she was ready.

Lord, but it felt alien to be in proper clothes, after her daily uniform of jeans and T-shirts. She looked at the reflection staring back at her and remembered that this was the image that had been *her* only a matter of a few short weeks ago.

In fact, this was one of her favourite dresses. One she had worn on a number of occasions to see her friends or go to the cinema. Casual but not too casual, revealing, but not alarmingly so, just sufficient to show off the length and shapeliness of her legs. The dark green hues complemented her colouring and the fairly prim style was compensated for by the way the fabric clung to her curves. If she was going to go to this damned local dance, then she certainly wasn't going to hide behind something unshapely and dull.

She had already bathed and dressed Simon. She had spoken to Maria on the phone two days previously, had immediately felt comfortable, and the day before Maria had popped over to the Rectory on her way to town so that she could meet the little boy who would be her charge for two hours at the most.

Sara had almost asked her whether she could confirm that her son had gone but the question would have sounded odd and she had cravenly shied away from mentioning his name just in case *that kiss* had been reported back to his mother.

But she had liked what she had seen and so had Simon.

Maria Dalgleish was very much like James to look at, apart from the eyes, and she looked feisty enough, but there was none of the arrogance or the casually assumed self-assurance that sat on her son's shoulders like a cloak.

She had arranged to drive over and was curious to see what this manor looked like and exactly how extensive those gardens were, when the doorbell went.

She pulled open the door, a ready smile on her face, her mouth half-open to tell Maria that she shouldn't have come for Simon, that she was going to drop him off herself as arranged.

Her smile froze as did her thought processes as she took in the man standing in front of her.

James Dalgleish, the man who should safely be miles away in London, the man who had managed to do what no other man had since Simon had been born, namely destabilise her, reach behind the fortress she had erected around herself and touch a part of her that did not want to be touched.

Tall, so beautiful that it brought a gasp to her throat and every inch a man she did not need in her life, not in any way, shape or form.

CHAPTER FOUR

'YOU! What are *you* doing here! You should be in London!'

'Oh, should I?' Dark, winged eyebrows shot up in apparent surprise at this statement, but surprised he most certainly was not. She would have thought he was in London, at least if she had wandered into the town again, and she undoubtedly would have had to, just as she would undoubtedly have had to have seen someone who would have started chatting to her, trying to find out what was going on between him and her. And it wouldn't have taken her long to discover that, as far as everyone was concerned, he had done his usual vanishing trick, because that was what his mother had told her friends, who would have told everyone else.

He had only found out by accident, having volunteered to drive his mother into town to meet her cronies for their weekly game of bridge.

'Oh, no need,' his mother had responded with uncustomary vagueness. 'I may have mentioned that you were heading back to the City, and why see them again just yet if you do not have to? Hm? You know the questions you will be asked! They can be so forthright sometimes.'

'You *may* have mentioned it, *cara Mama*?'

'It is possible, *sì*. I do not know. I cannot quite remember. Such a small detail!'

But actually having her believe that he was not around, that he wouldn't threaten her by being at the dance, suited him perfectly. James Dalgleish was not a man who hid behind neatly contrived preconceptions. She challenged him and he wanted her. Before he had laid eyes on her, his one thought had been the swift acquisition of the Rectory, to which end he had been prepared to do anything. Pay over the odds, find the woman somewhere else to live even if it meant building a house for her. He had enough money to compensate her in any way she chose, financially. Then he met her and for a while he saw himself as simply a shrewd businessman who was prepared to get to know his quarry, find out exactly whether her plans to live at the Rectory were long-term, discover the weakness that would provide him with what he wanted.

But he hadn't kicked off with his plan to denigrate the house, had he? And now he acknowledged that he just wanted her. Wanted to take her to his bed and make love to her, watch her closed, defensive face open up before his eyes like a flower blooming under the rays of the sun. He wanted to hear her moan aloud with desire, desire for *him*, he wanted to watch her writhe on his bed and lose all her inhibitions. All thoughts of buying the Rectory had temporarily taken a back seat to urges that were stronger and far, far more irresistible.

So the accusation burning in her eyes now was hardly a shock to his system.

'I was under the impression that you had urgent work to attend to in London!'

James shrugged and gave her a helplessly apologetic grimace that did nothing to erase the dismay she felt at seeing him again. And every pulse in her body was racing. She looked around a little desperately for Simon and called him, turning away so that she didn't have to look at the man lounging in front of her.

He was dressed in pale cream chinos that accentuated the lithe narrowness of his hips and the length of his legs,

and a dark grey short-sleeved shirt. Both reeked of im-
maculate and very pricey tailoring and neither did much
to lessen the predatorial impact of his darkly handsome
face and whipcord-lean body.

Now she felt hugely self-conscious in her get-up. She
had dressed to make a positive statement when she con-
fronted the people who were her neighbours, at least for
the moment. If you're whispering about me behind my
back, she wanted to imply, then you don't frighten me.

Instead, with those riveting dark blue eyes broodingly
looking at her, all she could feel was the straining of the
fine material of her dress against her breasts and the over-
exposure of her legs, which weren't even protected with
tights because the night was so balmy and she had predicted that it would be positively hot in the village hall.

She breathed a sigh of relief when she heard Simon's
little feet pattering towards the kitchen.

'Did your mother send you to fetch me?' Sara asked in
a stilted voice, clutching at the last straw that he might not
actually be going to the wretched dance. She bent down
to adjust her son's pyjama top and then ran her fingers
through his fine hair. 'Because there was no need. I'm
pretty sure I could find your house if it's next door to mine.
In fact,' she continued, standing up and clutching Simon's
hand in hers, 'it might be a good idea for me to follow
you in my car. I want to have my own transport.' In the
face of his silence, which was accompanied by a patient
tilt of his head, as if he was listening carefully to what she
was saying but not really paying a great deal of notice,
Sara felt herself chattering on witlessly. She gave a nervous laugh. 'I wouldn't want to find that I had to walk
home if I was having a rotten time! All this isolation
stretching into infinity! I would get hopelessly lost!' Her

voice faltered into silence and the silence continued for a few awkward seconds longer.

'I wouldn't dream of allowing you to go on your own,' James drawled, turning towards his car and expecting her to follow him.

'Don't be ridiculous!' She hesitated in front of the door, which he was holding open for her. 'I'm perfectly capable of getting myself to the town and finding where I should be going!'

'Nonsense.' He smiled implacably and, while she felt inclined to stand her ground and argue the matter till the cows came home, Simon removed the decision from her hands by opening the back car door and clambering into the seat.

The smile James gave her made her scowl.

'Do you *always* get your own way?' she snapped, sliding past him into the passenger seat and pressing her legs together.

'Always,' he assured her, half turning to look at her. 'You look stunning, by the way.' His mouth curved into a smile that sent a little thrill racing down her spine. 'But don't feel obliged to thank me for the compliment.'

'I won't,' Sara returned, instantly regretting her reply because it was unnecessary. 'But thank you anyway,' she added, turning to stare straight ahead.

'I brought my teddy,' Simon piped up from behind. 'Will Mrs…Mrs Babysitter mind?'

'I think she would love to see your teddy.' James started the engine and allowed Sara to stare frozenly ahead at the scenery while he chatted with her son. All that ice, but he had tasted those lips, had felt a surge of heat come from her straight into him and he knew that under the ice lay a hot pool of fire just waiting for him to ignite.

As they turned left and began the drive up to the manor,

Sara couldn't hold on to her pointed silence any longer. Her mouth dropped open as she took in the length, breadth and width of the rolling estate.

'This isn't all *yours*, is it?' she gasped, turning to stare at his averted profile.

'All of it,' he confirmed, a little nettled by the fact that his property impressed her, even if he didn't. 'Over there, to the right, there's a rose garden and even a miniature maze.'

Sara stared at the gracious manor rising up with effortless grace, dominating the courtyard which sprawled around a magnificent circular flower bed that was bursting with colour. A silver Rolls-Royce was parked neatly in front of the house.

'Is it a castle?' Simon breathed, awestruck, standing up so that he was peering between them with his teddy clutched in his arms.

'Not quite,' James said, laughing. 'Not uncomfortable enough.'

'And your mother lives here *on her own*?' Sara asked. The pale gold frontage seemed to stretch on forever, rising in places to turrets that belonged to something from a fairy tale.

'She has staff, naturally.'

'Oh, naturally,' Sara said, missing the amused look he threw at her. 'It must be awfully lonely for her.' They got out of the car and Sara stared upwards at the imposing façade. 'Rattling around here on her own, even if there *are* staff.'

'I come up and see her at least once a month,' James grated, not caring for the description of his mother *rattling around* in the house and caring even less for the assumption that she must be lonely.

'And then there are two of you rattling around.' Simon

tugged at her hand and she let herself be pulled towards the heavy oak door. 'Didn't you ever think of selling? Maybe buying something smaller for your mother? I would, if it were me.'

In that split instant he knew how she would react if he admitted that he had indeed thought of buying somewhere smaller and that the place he had in mind was only a stone's throw away, was in fact the Rectory which she had only just occupied.

She was wary enough of him already. In fact, she positively bristled with uneasy suspicion whenever he was within striking distance of her. Hearing that he wanted her house was not exactly going to fill her with trusting warmth, was it? Lust or cold-headed practicality? he wondered.

His eyes slid across to the long column of her neck as she gazed upwards, pale and beckoning in the mellow light of the evening sun.

Cold-headed practicality, he thought, would be dealt with later. It wouldn't be a problem. But it was not in his nature to issue an outright lie and so he cleverly evaded the question.

'This is our heritage,' he told her truthfully enough. 'And I would never sell it. It belongs to the Dalgleish family as it always will.' No lie there. His intentions weren't to sell the family home, merely convert it into something else, something that would do justice to its grandeur. 'Now, let's go inside.' He lightly placed his hand on her elbow and so engrossed was she in her surroundings that she barely noticed.

'Can I see the trains as soon as we get inside?' Simon asked hopefully.

'I hope he'll be OK—he's pretty much better now—but

he has been so ill with that chest infection—' Sara looked worriedly at James.

'I have my mobile phone. You can be contacted and be back here within half an hour. Surely this is what happened when you went out in London?'

'It was different there,' Sara said quickly. 'Lizzie knew him from birth, knew what to do if he got sick.' She had had to, Sara thought regretfully. Working long hours had necessitated that and long hours were what she had had to do to pay for the mortgage because Phillip's idea of maintenance had only ever been the very occasional flamboyant present for his son. And in the past two years, not even that.

As far as Phillip had been concerned, she had chosen to have the baby and so she could damn well take care of him financially herself. He was over-committed as it was with his apartment in London and a house in Portugal. When he had had the nerve to imply that she might have got herself pregnant as a passport to a wedding ring, Sara had ceased to talk about maintenance and done everything within her power to make sure that she took care of herself and her son to the best of her ability.

'Lizzie?'

'His nanny.'

'You had a nanny?'

'I had to work. There are such things as a mortgage, bills, food, clothes. Little things that usually have price tags attached to them.' She knew that she was being ridiculously defensive as all her old guilt rose to the surface and not for the first time. Guilt at having got pregnant in the first place, guilt at having to work, guilt at the hours she worked because being a top commodities trader had never been a nine-to-five job. So much guilt that she could drown under it if she let herself.

She was relieved when they were inside the house and Maria was with them, clucking over Simon, warmly asking Sara questions about what she thought of their town and tartly telling her son that his choice of colours did nothing for him, that he should have worn something a little less severe, considering they would be going to a casual little barbecue, some nice little checked shirt that didn't make him look as if he was taking a few hours' break from work.

'I don't *have* any checked shirts.'

Sara slid a sidelong glance at him and her mouth twitched at the cornered expression on his face.

'I look fine,' he muttered, looking pointedly at his watch.

'And do *you* agree?'

Sara found two pairs of eyes focused on her, one dark, the other navy blue and a lot more disconcerting. She chose to meet the dark pair.

'He looks all right,' she conceded.

'*All right?*' He couldn't help it. He did not consider himself by any means vain, but he was used to being seen as somewhat more than *all right. All right* was a pedestrian description to be applied to a pedestrian man and he struggled to contain a ludicrous feeling of pique in the face of those green eyes which were now doing a more detailed inventory of him.

'The shirt *is* a little on the sombre side, colour-wise,' Sara elaborated, unable to resist having a go, even if it was a very small one. It was just so satisfying to dent that massive ego of his. 'Not very summery, if you know what I mean, but I guess not bad.'

'Well,' he smiled slumberously, his blue eyes roving over her in a mimicry of her own physical appraisal of him except taking far, far longer, lingering over the pert swell of her breasts, the slenderness of her waist and the length

of her naked legs, 'then I should be thankful that you will
relieve the dullness of my clothing, shouldn't I?' He did
another leisurely appraisal of her, this time starting with
her feet and working upwards until he was looking at her
flushed face with lazy amusement.

'Now off you go, children.' Maria positively hustled
them to the front door. 'Simon and I want to play with a
certain set of trains before he gets too sleepy!'

'I won't be long and I'll take him home as soon as we
get back.'

'He will be sleeping!'

'He won't wake up. He sleeps like a log.'

'He can sleep the night here,' Maria said, frowning.
'There are more than enough bedrooms to accommodate
one small boy.' She smiled. 'And you as well, if you don't
want to spend the night away from him. Now, you run
along the both of you.'

Sara hovered uncertainly then bent to give Simon a hug.
When she stooped, her dress rode even higher up her
thighs. The statement outfit was proving to be a liability.

'There's no need to worry about him,' James soothed
as soon as they were in the car with the manor house
diminishing behind them. 'My *mama* loves children, like
all Italians. Left to her, I would have a dozen children so
that she could spend her time bustling around them.'

Sara slid a glance at him and couldn't imagine a less
likely candidate for a dozen children.

'Then why don't you oblige her?'

'I will…when the time is right.'

'And if it hasn't been right so far, then haven't you
asked yourself whether it ever will? Maybe there's a pat-
tern there. Never the right time in the right place for the
right woman.'

'The right woman…hm…interesting concept… You

mean I should stop dating blonde bimbos and look for another kind of woman to warm my bed?' His attempt to lighten the conversation went down like a lead balloon.

'Oh, no,' Sara said coolly, 'you just need to find the right blonde bimbo. She's out there somewhere!' She couldn't help it. She gave a bitter, sarcastic laugh and felt the sting of tears press against her eyelids.

'Tell me about your job.' The road straight ahead led almost directly to the village hall. James took the first left so that he could get there by the most circuitous route. 'What did you do in London?'

'I…I was a commodities trader.' Sara could almost hear the silence of surprised disapproval ricocheting around the car. 'And before you tell me that that was no kind of job for a woman, I might as well let you know that I was very good at it. More than that, it paid very well, which happens to be extremely handy when you're bringing up a child.'

'I can see why you needed a nanny,' was all he said. 'Commodity trading is an exhausting job. I don't suppose you got to see your son as much as you would have liked.'

The gentle sympathy in his voice caught her unawares and she found herself floundering between resentment at his observations and an overpowering urge to pour out her feelings. She had become so accustomed to carrying the weight of single motherhood on her shoulders, to pushing on however tired or depressed or just plain fed up she might be, that confiding in other people was a talent she had lost a long time ago. Even her girlfriends had not been privy to her innermost thoughts. She'd met them whenever they could arrange to, which was infrequently because most of them worked in the same high-octane field as she had, and they chatted about bonuses, holidays, frustrations at work but seldom about how they really felt. They were all young, in enviably well-paid jobs, they had no time to be depressed. They laughed, ate at expensive restaurants and veered away from anything that might imply that their lifestyles were not all that they were cracked up to be.

'I suppose you think that I was an irresponsible mother, bringing a child into the world and then not even spending any quality time with him, but I had no choice. Trading was the only thing I was good at. I didn't go to university, I was a hopeless secretary. I would have been fired sooner or later if my boss didn't happen to notice that I had an ability to predict market trends. And trading is a game you can't slow down without getting left behind.' She could hear the pitch of her voice rising in defensiveness and took a few deep, steadying breaths. 'Are we nearly there?'

'Nearly.'

She waited for him to continue trying to drag information out of her and was half hoping that he would because in the darkness of the car it felt good to talk, like being in a confessional, but he didn't. He just pointed out one or two landmarks to her and then prosaically began to talk about places she could visit, things Simon might like to see when they got a chance.

Why wasn't he talking about *her*? she wondered feverishly. For a minute there she had actually thought that he was genuinely interested, genuinely sympathetic to what she had gone through for the past five years, and there was a dam inside her waiting to burst. But suddenly he had stopped asking questions, lost all interest.

As soon as he had heard what she had done for a living, Sara thought slowly. She had been so right to bracket James Dalgleish and Phillip in the same category. Neither of them had really liked a woman who possessed an intellect that could threaten them. Phillip had slept with her because she had been a novelty for him and because he had liked the way she looked, but where was he now?

Getting married and moving to Sydney. Getting married to a woman who was blonde, helpless and had never done a day's hard work in her life. Getting married to a woman who was seven months pregnant. She herself had not seen her ex for nearly nine months and her friends had been all too willing to explain why. She suspected even he might have felt some twinge of feeling for her and the son he had never really acknowledged. In due course, a letter would arrive and there would be one line of regret for the way things turned out but rather more than one somehow laying the blame for everything at her door, and a good deal more devoted to how he had finally found what he had been looking for all his life. The letter would arrive to a flat occupied by tenants and she sincerely hoped that they would drop it in the nearest bin. She detested Phillip, but rejection still hurt and what hurt even more was knowing that her son had been rejected as well.

By the time they reached the village hall, her mood had sunk to rock-bottom. She could barely look at the man walking in with her, and when he brushed against her arm as they entered she visibly flinched.

Thankfully there was no need to stay glued to his side. Fiona had turned up and was waving at her from across the room, and the sea of hostility and suspicion she thought she would find was absent. Everyone was too busy having a good time. The music was loud and operated by an enthusiastic youth with shoulder-length hair and there was a long buffet table extending across one side of the hall, on which she assumed food would be laid out in due course.

It was as far removed from a fashionable London night-club as it was possible to get.

'I'll get you a drink,' James said into her ear. 'Stay here.' He moved away into the crowd, stopping every two feet to have a few words with someone, and Sara immediately headed towards Fiona.

Stay here? Did he imagine that he could issue imperatives and she would mindlessly obey? Out of the corner of her eye, she could see him still trying to get to the bar, where three middle-aged gentlemen were trying to keep up with the crowd of people putting in their orders, and she smirked with satisfaction at the thought of him returning to that spot by the door to find that she had disappeared into the crowd. Of course, it wouldn't be long before he zeroed in on her, but by then she would have proved her point.

If this had been London, she thought with another of those pangs of regret, she could well and truly have lost herself. The crowds and the darkness of a nightclub would have easily swallowed her up. Not so here. They had dimmed the lights but dark it certainly was not and the crowds couldn't hide a fly for more than twenty minutes.

And if she had been with her friends…but she wouldn't have been with her friends at a nightclub. They would have been at a smart wine bar or an expensive restaurant, swapping anecdotes about who was doing what at work, and at the back of her mind guilt would have been nagging away that she had left Simon at night when she had been out all day. At least here she didn't feel guilty about leaving him with Maria for a couple of hours. They had had a good day together, doing some weeding, baking some bread, taking time out to just sit in the garden where she had sleepily watched him play with his Lego on a rug while she read a magazine. Little, simple things that her friends would never have understood because they belonged to a fervently child-free culture and talk of children bored them.

Fiona and her three friends all had children and it was

weird to discuss Simon openly without seeing only polite interest on their faces. It was even interesting to discuss schooling in the area when she knew full well that the chances of their staying put was only fifty-fifty, if that.

She felt his approach before she saw him. Even in a crowded room, with disco music rattling out in the background, she still felt his approach. It made the hairs on the back of her neck stand on end and she steeled herself for his inevitable remark about walking off when he had pointedly told her to stay put.

She was aggrieved to find that he was glaringly indifferent to whether she had walked off, stayed put or even headed back in the direction of home.

He handed her a glass of wine, which she drank with record speed, and then ignored her while he chatted amicably with her companions. Fiona tried to include her in the conversation while her bright eyes darted between the two of them, taking in their body language. But their histories went back a long way. Mutual friends were mentioned, incidents referred to, and after a while Sara excused herself to get some more wine. Two glasses and she was feeling much better.

'Not running away from me by any chance?' His velvety voice washed over her and she turned to him with a radiant smile.

'Don't look now but your ego's showing,' Sara said smugly, happily accepting her third glass of wine. A pleasant contentment washed over her. 'Not surprising, though, considering that all the lassies are fluttering their eyelashes at you.'

'So you've been watching me, have you?' His gaze swept over her with lazy speculation. It gave him a kick of satisfaction to think that she had been following his progress through the room, looking at every woman he had stopped to talk to. Her green eyes were glittering up at him, amazing eyes, like green glass. He raised his glass to his lips and continued to stare at her upturned face until she reddened, although, he noticed, she didn't tear her gaze away as she normally would, so that she could rush behind her defences. She met his stare and matched it.

'Of course I haven't been *watching you*.'

'Well, I've been watching you,' he said softly, 'along with most of the other unattached males in this place. Would you like to dance?'

Before she could formulate an answer, he had circled her waist with his hands and was pulling her in the direction of the makeshift dance floor.

Her soft compliance as she leant into him made him tighten the muscles around his loins and a hot wave of unexpectedly primitive emotion flooded through him. He tightened his hold on her, pulling her closer into him so that he could feel the crush of her soft breasts against his chest and so that she could feel the hardness between his legs that would be telling her exactly what he wanted to do with her.

'People will talk,' Sara murmured, allowing her head to rest lightly on his shoulder.

'Because we're dancing?' He knew exactly what she meant. It wasn't that they were dancing, but how they were dancing. There was not a millimetre of space between them and she was gyrating slowly against his body, in time to the slow, steady beat of the love song.

Lord, but was this how she danced with other men? The thought sent a shard of searing jealousy straight through him and he curled his fingers into her long hair, tilting her face to his.

'Do you go to a lot of nightclubs in London, Sara?' he

asked huskily and she gave a low-throated gurgle of laughter and shook her head.

'I try and not go out at all. Or, at least, not very often. Sometimes on a Saturday evening, although Sundays were always the worst for me. Don't you find Sundays the loneliest day of the week?' She trailed her fingers from his shoulders to the back of his neck and he audibly caught his breath.

'How much have you had to drink?' he queried unsteadily.

'Three glasses. And counting.'

'Three glasses and full stop.'

'I hope you're not telling me how much I can drink, Mr Dalgleish, because if you are then I'm afraid you don't know me at all.'

'Because you don't take orders from a man?'

'That's right.' God, it had been a long time since she had danced like this with a man. Thinking about it, she didn't remember ever dancing like this with a man, not even Phillip, who had hated dancing anyway and was scathing of anywhere that loud music was played and he might be obliged to get up and dance.

'Now, that's something that might come between us,' he murmured lazily.

'Because you like ordering people about?'

'Because when I sleep with a woman I like to be in charge.'

His words floated over her and into her and then crashed through her consciousness, leaving behind a surge of excitement that made her nipples harden against the lacy covering of her bra.

'Are you hungry?'

'Wh...what?'

'Because I see they're beginning to put out the food over

there.' The music came to an abrupt halt, someone announced that food was served and that everyone had to form an orderly queue, and he pulled away from her.

Something in her stomach. She needed something in her stomach. She could feel the alcohol, precious little but more than she was used to drinking, swishing around inside her. The barbecue smelled delicious.

'It will sober you up,' James said in an undertone and when she was beginning to wonder whether the postscript to that remark was that, sober, she wouldn't carry on making a fool of herself, he continued with a lazy half-smile, 'so that I cannot later be accused of having had my wicked way with someone under the influence of drink.' His eyes tangled with hers.

'You won't be having your wicked way with me,' Sara protested weakly.

'Shall we join some of the others outside?' He had to stop looking at those drowsy, beckoning eyes or he would have no choice but to abandon eating and drag her somewhere private, to hell with what the entire town had to say on the subject. Corporate businesswoman she might well have been, but when it came to emotions she was the most intriguing woman he had ever met and the complex combination of vulnerability and gutsy intelligence was driving him crazy.

Sara was barely aware of the conversation swirling around her as she munched her way through chicken, a sausage and some bits of salad and bread. The only thing she was aware of was the energy emanating from the man sitting alongside her on the bench, his thigh grazing hers every so often.

When the music started back, drifting through the open windows to where outside lights had been switched on to accommodate the gathering darkness, James stood up and announced that it was time for them to leave.

'Sara wants to be back early as it's the first time my mother is babysitting her son.'

Her chance was now, to agree with him and leave, but to go where and do what, or to disagree, stand her ground and put her provocative behaviour down to a little too much wine on an empty stomach. Right now, she felt as sober as a judge.

Wrong time, wrong place and definitely, she thought, wrong man. She was behaving like a teenager instead of the responsible mother that she was, flopping all over him like a wet rag and acting as though that husky voice of his and his body pressing against hers so that she could feel his arousal was because of *her*. When instead he was only a red-blooded male responding in typical fashion to a reasonably attractive woman who had too much wine inside her for her own good.

But she had been in a deep freeze for five years. Somewhere along the line she had forgotten that she was only twenty-six, hardly over the hill.

'He can be a bit nervous with strangers, to start with,' Sara said, clearing her throat and standing up. 'I promised him that I wouldn't be back late. Where shall I put my plate and glass?'

'Leave it here,' Fiona said, catching her eye and grinning broadly. 'I'll take it in. Some of us poor, hapless souls have been roped into doing all the clearing away, so we'll be here until the break of dawn. Or at least until eleven-thirty when our resident DJ packs up and leaves.'

'That would be my brother,' Helen explained, smiling, 'and he'll pack up exactly when I tell him to.'

It was only when they were outside in the clear, cool air that a sickening rush of nerves washed over her, and when she stepped gingerly into his car it intensified to the point where she had to rest her head back and close her eyes.

He didn't start the engine immediately. Instead, he turned in his seat and looked at her. 'If you want to back out, tell me now.'

Sara slowly inclined her head so that she was looking straight into his glittering eyes. 'I don't know what to do,' she answered truthfully.

'I know what you *want* to do,' he murmured, reaching out to slide his fingers along her cheek and into her hair, and Sara's breath caught painfully in her throat.

'Where will we go?'

'To the Rectory.' He gave her a killing smile that made her shiver with fear and searing anticipation. 'And don't worry,' he dipped his fingers to her half-parted mouth and gently traced its outline, 'I'm not a beast. If you change your mind along the way, I won't take advantage of you.' But she wouldn't, he thought with a flare of triumph that made his loins physically ache. She wanted him as badly as he wanted her. He could feel it in the loaded atmosphere between them. The air was thick with unexpressed needs. He was not surprised when she gave him an imperceptible nod and only then did he turn away and fire the engine into life.

CHAPTER FIVE

EVEN to Sara's racing mind, the drive back seemed a lot shorter and was accomplished in silence. A silence pregnant with slick excitement.

'Changed your mind yet?' James asked softly, when they reached the Rectory and he had killed the engine.

'Changed yours?' She laughed a little wryly. 'We're behaving like teenagers. At least I am. It's just that...'

'Just that what...?'

'Oh, I don't know.' She shrugged and stared out of the window. Yes, she wanted to sleep with him. Badly. Too badly, and that was the problem, but how could she explain that to him? How could she tell him that she was frankly terrified of opening herself up to another man when her experiences with the last one had left her mortally wounded? He would roar with laughter. This wasn't about having a relationship as far as James Dalgleish was concerned, it was about having sex, and having sex was not something he would associate with agonising.

'Look, why don't we go inside and we can...talk?'

'Are you interested in talking?' She looked at him and he felt a sharp tug somewhere inside at the worried expression on her face. 'No, of course you're not,' she said on a little sigh. 'Why should you be? What does sex have to do with talking?'

'Come on.' He slung open his car door and strode round so that he could pull hers open for her. 'If you need to talk until this time next week, then I'm going to listen, so out you come and we'll go inside and get ourselves some good, strong coffee.'

'You don't have to...I know the last thing you want to do is drink coffee at a kitchen table and chat, especially when...especially since...'

He didn't answer. Instead he took her limp hand in his and gently pulled her out of the car.

'Where are your keys?'

'I can open the door.' She detached her hand from his so that she could rummage around in her bag, and as soon as she had found the keys and opened the side-door immediately wanted to slip her hand back into his.

No wonder I'm in a state, she thought jerkily. When was the last time she had wanted physical contact with a man? But what the hell must he be thinking of her? She certainly wasn't living up to her image of a savvy London girl who had moved in the fast lane and knew how to behave accordingly. She was acting like an adolescent suffering an extreme case of first-date nerves.

'There's no need...'

'If you say that once more, I'll throttle you. Now step aside, and go into the kitchen. I'll make us some coffee and we can take it into the sitting room. Then we'll...talk.' He leaned against the frame of the door, towering over her, and she stood back to let him brush past.

'Perhaps we should go back to your house. I need to check and make sure that Simon's OK.'

'He'll be fine.' He stuck the kettle on, fetched mugs, spooned coffee into them and resisted the temptation to turn around and drink in the figure on the chair. Having given him the green light, she was now applying the brakes as if her life depended on it, and to his amazement he wasn't in the slightest bit annoyed. Frustrated yes, but annoyed no. And he still wanted her. Instead of dampening his enthusiasm, her hesitant retreat seemed to have fuelled him even more. He must be mellowing with age, he thought with wry bemusement.

'Now, you go into the sitting room. You can call my mother and find out whether everything's all right, but she would have called me if there had been a problem. I took my mobile phone with me. Still, if it puts your mind at rest…'

'Why are you being so understanding?' Sara asked warily. 'And don't tell me that you're an understanding man by nature.'

'Well,' James shot her a slow, amused smile that made her stomach curl like a fist inside her, 'I must say I've never known any woman who's used aggression as part of her courtship routine.'

'We're not courting one another, though,' Sara returned quickly, 'so I'm allowed.' Courtship? James Dalgleish? Had he ever courted a woman in his life? She very much doubted it, and then hard on the heels of that thought came another—what would it be like? What would it be like to have this big, powerful, self-confident, sexy man go weak at the knees at the thought of a woman? To find himself unable to function unless she was around? The thought of it made her blush and she hustled towards the sitting room, acutely conscious of him following closely behind her.

'You can't hide away forever.' Those were his first words the minute she had sat down and he had moved across to the bay window so that he could perch against the ledge and stare down at her.

'Because I didn't jump into the sack with you doesn't mean that I'm hiding away from anything!' Sara lied, but there was no vigour in her voice. He was staring at her in

the same probing way that she would have shied away
from a day ago, but which now made her want to
just…just let him in. She had no idea where the urge was
coming from but her helplessness to fight it off frightened
her.

'Of course you are.' James sauntered towards the sofa
and sat down next to her, depressing it with his weight. It
was small enough for his thigh to rest lightly against hers
and all those crazy, racing pulses leapt into life as he
turned to look at her, stretching out his arm along the back
of the sofa so that it was resting loosely behind her shoulders. 'Why else would you have run out here, to the back
of beyond?'

'You know why. Simon…Simon has had these recurrent
chest infections for years; he needed to get out of London.
This house, coming when it did, just seemed like the hand
of fate.'

'You could have moved to the country and still been
within commuting distance of your job in London.'

'Why are you pinning me against the wall with your
questions?'

'Because you said you wanted to talk and talk you will.
What's the relationship with Simon's father?'

'What's that got to do with anything?' She began to look
away and he caught her chin in one hand and forced her
to look at him instead.

'Just about everything,' he grated. 'I want to sleep with
you, but I have no intention of sleeping with a woman
who's still involved with her ex.' It shocked him just how
much he hated the thought of someone else having a claim
to her body, to her mind.

'And here I was, thinking that you were one of those
typical, unscrupulous high-fliers,' Sara mocked in an at-

tempt to lighten the atmosphere. It didn't work. He continued to look at her with such unsmiling concentration that she felt giddy and the curling feeling in her stomach began to spread to other places in her body.

'You still haven't answered my question.'

'I don't *have* any kind of relationship with Phillip,' Sara said in a rush. Her cheeks were pink with colour. 'No, I'm lying. I have got a relationship with Phillip, but it's more along the lines of loathing.' She gave a bitter laugh. 'You could say we didn't part on the best of terms.'

'You mean before you came up here?'

'I mean when he discovered I was pregnant. There. Satisfied?'

'I'll tell you when I'm satisfied,' James murmured. 'And I'm not. I take it he didn't like the thought of becoming a daddy?'

'What's the point in talking about this?' Sara squirmed.

'The point is that you can't live your life if you're still attached to your past.'

'That's psychobabble.'

'Is it? I bet you haven't had a relationship with any man since Simon's been on the scene,' he said astutely. 'Have all the men in your life over the past five years just been good friends, Sara?'

Pride struggled with weary helplessness and she shrugged. 'You don't understand. You go out to work because you want to not because you have to. I've worked so that I could pay off the mortgage and raise a child. I haven't had a choice and there's no room to clock-watch when you're a commodity trader. It's not a nine-to-five job and just the smallest hint of weakness would have cost me my job. I haven't had…had time to devote to cultivating a relationship.' She found that she was wringing her hands together and she made an effort to still them.

'So you worked from dawn till dusk and spent your leisure time feeling guilty because you had to leave your son in the care of a stranger.'

'She wasn't a stranger,' Sara said, hearing the misery in her voice with distaste. Self-pity was an indulgence which she had always viewed with contempt, except in the very early hours of the morning, when the rest of the world was asleep and she could allow her mind to drift over its past and build castles that were never going to be.

'You could have got another job, something less demanding. Moved out of London, worked somewhere in one of the counties.'

'You don't understand,' Sara muttered, tugging her face out of his controlling grip so that she didn't have to look into those disturbing, piercing navy blue eyes.

She knew why he was doing this, sitting on this sofa, encouraging her to spill out her life history. He wanted to sleep with her and was prepared to help her over this little stumbling block simply as a means to an end. What confused her was her own temptation to yield. She had spent too long on her own, she thought feverishly, too long warding off the rest of the world. She had confided in Phillip and look where that had got her.

'So you keep telling me. Well, then, why don't you enlighten me?'

He watched the fractional tilt of her head and the stubborn compression of her mouth and thought that if he had any sense at all he would leave her to her zealously protected thoughts and walk right out of the kitchen door. He wasn't interested in playing lengthy games with the opposite sex.

'Scared, Sara?' he murmured softly. She didn't answer, just continued to stare unblinkingly in front of her. 'What did that bastard do to you?' he enquired and it was the gentleness in his voice that did it for her.

She felt the prick of tears behind her lids and was mortified when one oozed out of the corner of her eye.

'Sorry,' she mumbled, rubbing her fist against her eye and taking several deep breaths. He silently handed her a crisp white handkerchief and she dabbed her eyes without looking at him and then clenched the handkerchief in her hand. 'I bet you hate women who cry.'

He flushed darkly when she slid her eyes sideways to catch the expression of discomfort on his face.

'Thought so.'

'I don't hate women who cry, *per se*,' James said, wondering how he had suddenly happened to find himself on the back legs.

'You just hate it when they cry because they want more from you than you're prepared to give.'

'We weren't talking about *me*,' he rasped uncomfortably and Sara impulsively reached out and stroked the side of his cheek. It was the first time she had glimpsed any loss of that phenomenal self-control and he suddenly looked like a boy, caught having to confess to something he didn't want to.

James caught her hand in his and nipped her soft palm, looking into her face as he did so. 'Witch,' he murmured, 'don't think you can change the subject whenever you want to. I'm not through talking to you quite yet.' He trailed his tongue lightly against the soft underside of her wrist and she gasped at the burst of pleasure that the simple touch invoked.

Phillip had been her first and only lover but his lovemaking had been targeted towards his own satisfaction, something she had only seen in retrospect and with the advantage of hindsight when the limitations of his personality had become stunningly obvious. She had had no points of comparison but instinctively she knew that James was not cut from the same cloth. At least not as far as the sexual game was concerned.

She was breathing quickly as he trailed a leisurely path with his mouth along her arm, finally pulling her towards him so that he could assault her mouth in a kiss that was lingering and coaxing but ultimately promised total possession. Every pore in her body was screaming out for satisfaction.

'I…I thought you wanted…to talk.'

'Later. Now…shall we go somewhere more comfortable?' He paused to murmur against her mouth and Sara nodded drowsily at him.

'Upstairs. My bedroom. It's the first door on the left.' She found that she could barely utter the words coherently.

Before she could put her trembling legs to the test, he had reached out and scooped her up, carrying her through the sitting room as though she weighed less than a feather, then up the stairs and along the landing until he could nudge open the door to her bedroom with his foot.

'Please, no lights,' Sara begged, when he made to turn on the overhead light.

'I'll compromise,' he drawled by way of response, and promptly switched on the little lamp on the table by the side of the king-sized bed, so that the room was bathed in a very soft glow. 'I want to see you, my darling. I want to see your face when I touch you and I want you to see me.'

He watched her cheeks turn pink and marvelled how a

woman who had obviously held her own in the demanding, cut-throat world of trading could be rendered as shy as a kitten when it came to her own sexuality.

He had laid her on the bed and he looked at her as she stared at him with fascination, her red hair dramatic against the pale cream bed linen.

Deliberately he removed his clothes, item by item. First his shirt, then his shoes, his socks and his trousers, never letting his eyes leave her face. Her breath was coming in short little gasps. Did she know how much of a turn-on it was for him to be watched the way she was watching him now? he wondered. What was going on in her head? She didn't want to be attracted to him, had fought against it tooth and nail, but she was. So how valuable was his conquest? One part of her was his, but he was slowly discovering that capturing that one part was not going to be enough. It helped that she wasn't harbouring any nostalgic feelings about her ex, but he still wanted more than her physical capitulation.

He was thickly and impressively aroused when he stripped off his boxer shorts and he smiled with indolent amusement as her mouth parted at the sight of him.

She couldn't help it. She dazedly thought that his body was as much a work of art as it was possible for any human body to be. Broad-shouldered, with his powerful chest narrowing to a slim waist and hips and legs that no one in their right mind would ever have associated with a businessman. She could discern the flex of his muscles and sinews beneath the olive-toned skin, and when her eyes alighted on his proudly erect manhood she found that she couldn't tear them away.

He walked towards the side of the bed and extended his

hands, reaching out for her to take them so that he could draw her to her feet.

The thought of her naked body was something to be savoured. He wanted to be the one who removed her clothes, so that he could see her nudity inch by inch, appreciate every tiny bit of it in slow degrees.

He unzipped the dress from the back and she arched as he kissed the slender column of her neck, then her shoulders as the dress was tugged down to her waist, exposing her breasts straining through the lacy bra.

Later. He would savour them later, feast on them, but for now he was content to span her waist with his big hands and draw her close so that he could take her mouth in a lingering kiss.

She was tall and slender, just the opposite of the small, voluptuous women he had always favoured, but there was something unbearably erotic about the sensuous length of her, the perfect flawlessness of her pale skin.

He brought his hands up to cup her breasts and she sighed with pleasure, automatically pushing them towards him, conducting her own inventory of his body with her hands. She ran them along his shoulders, then circled his tight brown nipples with her thumbs, then moved to caress the hard, flat planes of his stomach.

She was wearing too many clothes. She wanted to feel him, flesh against flesh, and as if the need was as strong in him as it was in her he dragged down her dress, which fell to her ankles, allowing her to step out of it.

'Now, bed…'

'What about the rest of my clothes?' Sara asked, dipping her eyes at the naked yearning in his expression.

'Oh, don't worry, I shall get to that…'

There was something shamelessly wanton about lying

semi-clothed on a vast bed, with a big man towering possessively over you. Sara smiled with half-closed eyes, inviting his ravishing appraisal of her, which was no less searing than the one she was affording him.

There was no yesterday and no tomorrow, only this moment, right here and now, timeless.

Sara pushed herself up against the pillows and reached behind with trembling fingers to unclasp the bra. Sensation was racing through her, betraying every line of defence she had ever adopted when it came to the opposite sex. She just knew that she wanted this man's eyes on her and his hands on her and his body to possess hers utterly.

James moved towards the side of the bed and lowered himself alongside her, watching her quivering body and relishing the thought of tasting every last inch of it. As her bra was undone and before she could pull it off, he straddled her so that his length covered hers and he supported himself on his elbow as he slipped his free hand under the bra to cup the soft mound of her breast.

He felt her low moan as he began teasing one nipple, rolling it gently between his thumb and forefinger. He nudged up the bra and feasted on the sight of her bare breasts. Lord, but he would have to control his urge to take her immediately, right now, and release the pounding, physical ache of his desire in his loins.

He lay over her and caught his hands in her hair. Her head was flung back and another moan escaped her as he traced her lower lip with his tongue, then tasted the sweetness of her mouth in a slow, sensual kiss that had her writhing like a cat beneath him.

It had been a long time, and even when she had made love all that time ago it had never been like this. Through her hazy mind, she knew that she was being touched by a man who had complete mastery in the art of making love. His mouth was demanding and hungry yet delicately lingering and she was so absorbed with the pleasure of it that she was hardly aware that he had nudged apart her thighs, the better for her to feel his rampant maleness pressed against her. He moved slowly over her, his hard shaft pressing against her moist cleft with an evocative rhythm that made her gasp.

'Enjoying yourself, *cara*?'

'You…you know I am.'

'Then why don't you tell me?'

'Don't stop. Please.'

Her words sent fierce adrenaline rushing through him. He slid off the bra and eased himself lower so that he could trace the tight bud of her swollen nipple with the tip of his tongue, and when she could bear it no longer she tangled her fingers into his hair and pushed him down so that he could suckle on her nipple and draw it shamelessly into his mouth.

A groan escaped her and her voice, so husky that she barely recognised it as her own, pleaded with him to take her. Her briefs were wet with her unbidden arousal, she could feel it, and when he eased them off she quivered with relief and instinctively parted her legs, inviting his entrance.

But he wasn't ready. He shifted his attention from one breast to the other, teasing the full pink disc with his mouth while his hand trailed down to her stomach and navel, then with inexorable slowness to the slippery crease between her thighs.

Sara tensed as he probed and then rubbed the sensitive clitoris that had her releasing her breath in shaky gasps as if she was fighting for air.

She was perched on the edge of orgasm, then she was free falling, unable to resist the powerful shudders of soaring pleasure as he continued to rub her before easing his finger deep into her moistness. Her body literally shook and trembled under the assault of sensation, and when she finally stilled she could barely open her eyes to look at him.

He would be disappointed but she had been powerless to resist his stimulation. She groaned with frustration and looked at him.

'I'm sorry,' Sara whispered and he smiled at her.

'What for?' He lay next to her on his side and turned her to face him.

'For...for...you know why...' As if to demonstrate what she found difficult to say, she touched him and his hardness pulsed in response.

'You don't think that we've finished already, do you?'

Green eyes widened.

'I've only explored a part of your body,' he informed her with a low, sexy laugh.

As if to prove his point, he raised her arm and proceeded to trace a path with his lips along her side, reawakening ripples of sensation in her. Then he moved his attention to her stomach, to the soft indentation of her navel, then down to the most intimate place of all, where his skilful fingers had just finished their masterful assault.

'No!' Sara tried to clamp shut her legs, but without success.

'No?' He looked up at her, then, to further addle her, he blew gently against the still swollen nub of her femininity. 'Why not?'

'You can't...I've never...'

'Never had a man's mouth down there?' The shockingly

forthright question had her blushing furiously and she would have bucked against him but it would have been useless. His weight was rendering her immobile. 'There's a first time for everything, though, isn't there?'

Without allowing the chance for debate, he lowered his head and with almost unbearable delicacy touched the tip of her clitoris with his tongue.

From feeling spent only minutes previously, Sara's body charged into life as if a jolt of electricity had run through it. Where she would have writhed, he held her still with his hands firmly placed on her hips. Then he was licking with a rhythmic pressure that had her groaning with undisguised rapture.

She had never reached these heights before and her whole body was trembling with a rippling onslaught of sensations that had her crying out.

Then when she thought, anguished, that she would again no longer be able to restrain herself from capitulating to what he was doing to her body, he was breaking away from the honeyed moistness and moving to cover her body with his in one fluid movement.

'Contraception,' he murmured and her eyes flickered open at the prosaic nature of the remark.

'Wh…what?'

'Are you using any?' he questioned softly, 'because if you aren't, then there are other ways of…reaching a climax without penetration…'

He was responsible, her brain registered dimly, responsible enough to think about the consequences of what they were about to do. She half smiled. 'There's no need to worry,' she said, stretching up, feline-like, to coil her arms around his shoulders. 'And no need to talk either,' she whispered.

In actual fact, she was on the Pill, not because her sex life required it, but because the Pill regulated her periods and helped to lighten the flow. The explanation was there if he wanted it, but right now she wasn't intending to launch into it. Her body was screaming for fulfilment and she could tell from the glitter in his eyes that he was as well.

Sara felt him enter her and her body tensed as every muscle stretched to accommodate his size. He eased himself in slowly, withdrew slightly, eased himself further in and then he was moving inside her, deep thrusts that had her spiralling towards the most powerful climax she had ever experienced.

And she witnessed his own soaring passion as his powerful body arched back on one long, final thrust and he shuddered to complete fulfilment.

He could have made love to her again. He wanted nothing more than to lose himself once more in her exquisite body and let her lose herself in his, but there was a thread of uncertainty running through him that made him wonder whether she would just pull back, retreat again to a place where he might not be able to reach her.

He had wanted her and now he felt himself consumed by the possibility of having her again. His vague plan to somehow get to know her so that he could manoeuvre his way into buying the Rectory lay in splinters at his feet, but he didn't care. At least not at this moment in time. At this moment in time the only thing he cared about was repeating the mind-blowing experience they had shared.

'We...we have to go and collect Simon,' was the first coherent thing that came to her mind as he lay on his side and tugged her so that she was facing him.

'It's...' he glanced at the clock on the mantelpiece over

the fireplace '…eleven-fifteen. He'll be asleep already…' He didn't want to scare her off but just lying here next to her was making his body stir into life once again. 'So he won't notice whether you're there now or…in an hour's time…and I can think of other things we can do to fill the time…' He stroked the side of her breast then rolled one nipple between his fingers, feeling a flare of triumph as it hardened at his touch.

Sex. It was all about sex, and she honestly couldn't blame him. They had made love like people who had spent years starved of physical contact. Right in her case, but in his case? He was just a highly skilled lover who knew how to press the right buttons to get the right responses.

'No,' she said weakly, disturbed by the thought that there should be something more than just the act of making love, however glorious that was in itself.

'Why not?' He removed his hand and she felt the loss of contact with a shiver of dismay.

'Because…because we just can't.'

'Can't…?'

Sara twisted her head so that she didn't have to look into his eyes. Those eyes made her doubt everything she had ever believed, made her wonder whether shying away from men so that she could never be hurt had actually been such a good idea after all. She didn't want to doubt herself. She had Simon to consider. There was no way that she would expose him to having a man around, only for the man to disappear just as his own father had. And James Dalgleish was a disappearing kind of man. You didn't need a degree in rocket science to spot that a mile off.

'I need to get dressed.'

'Oh, no, you don't.' He gripped her arm firmly enough to anchor her to the spot but not so hard that he was physically hurting her, although she knew that the slightest attempt by her to get off the bed would result in enough pressure for him to ensure that she went nowhere.

'How long do you plan on running away, Sara? Another year? Two years? The rest of your life?'

'You're hurting my arm.'

'*Por Dios,* woman! We all screw up once in a while! The trick is not to end up haunted by it!' He could feel her withdrawing with every passing second and his powerlessness to do anything about it made him want to break things. But aggression would get him nowhere. He forced himself to calm down, released her arm and gave her a long, measured look.

'*You've* screwed up? *Ever?*'

'Yes, if you must know.' He felt as if he was stepping off the edge of something, but *what*...? 'When I was young, I had a fling with a woman ten years older than me. I thought it was love until I surprised her at her flat one afternoon with another man. Turned out I was a little plaything being cultivated by the pair of them as an easy route to some quick cash. Marry me, divorce me, end up rich. Nice, quick, foolproof.' There was no reason why he should have kept this untold story to himself, but it still confused the hell out of him as to why he had felt so damned compelled to tell it in the first place.

'What did you do?'

'I learnt my lesson,' he said abruptly.

'But you didn't have a child.'

'No.'

'And children get hurt.'

'And adults can use that to hide behind!'

'I want to get my son back now.' Her heart was beating like a drum and something inside her head was screaming out to her that one wrong move now would land her waist-deep in quicksand.

'Feel free.' He lay back with his hands behind his head.

'What do you mean, *feel free*?'

'I mean feel free to go and get him. I'll be waiting right here till you get back.'

'Why is it so hard for you to take no for an answer?' Sara flared in sudden anger. She swept her legs off the bed and stormed towards the bathroom, clutching her bundle of clothes in one hand.

OK, so maybe she shouldn't have slept with him, but she had and she didn't regret one minute of it. She just didn't want it to go any further. Why couldn't he accept that?

She had a very quick shower, changed and half expected that he would have left but when she returned to the bed-room it was to find that he was still there, although thank-fully back in his clothes and lounging against the bay win-dow.

'I'll be waiting right here for you,' he informed her steadily.

'Why?' The question was torn from her.

'Because we want one another and it's no good pre-tending otherwise. You're not some virginal maiden in ter-ror of a rampant male, you're just someone who's ready to close the whole world out as a self-inflicted punishment because you made a mistake a long time ago.'

'And having hundreds of relationships is as bad as hav-ing none! The truth is that you enjoyed a romp in the hay and now you'd quite like to enjoy a couple more, hence your apparent need to climb into my mind and point out all the things you think I'm doing wrong!' She burned at the memory of how good sex with him had been and how easy it would be to carry on hopping into bed for just as long as he wanted her, just to repeat the glorious feelings he had aroused in her. How easy it would be to let him into her life and into Simon's. 'You're not exactly trying to understand me from a purely unbiased point of view, are you?'

His eyes narrowed at her. 'Do you know what you need?' he asked, moving so slowly towards her that she could easily have yanked open the bedroom door and fled down the stairs. However, her legs appeared to have turned to lead and she stood just where she was, only managing to shuffle a few steps backwards until her back was pressed against the door. He stopped inches away from her and then proceeded to place the flat of his palms on either side of her. 'You need to be shaken into seeing sense.'

The thudding of her heart became a steady, painful drum roll.

'Why don't you stop hiding away and face facts? We're both adults who happen to be attracted to one another. Overwhelmingly attracted,' he added as an afterthought. He traced her bare arm with his finger and she shivered convulsively. 'See? Your mouth might be saying one thing but your body is telling a completely different story. Like me to prove it?'

'No!' Sara squeaked, mesmerised by his eyes.

In some obscure part of his brain, he realised that this was his only trump card. For a while, she had abandoned the hold her past had on her, but all the old defences were back, except one. She couldn't defend herself against his touch. He had never chased a woman in his life before, but, dammit, he was prepared to do anything to chase this one. He didn't know why. He just knew that there was a raw, primitive urge in him that wanted her…badly.

'You're scared of a relationship and I'm not interested in one, and maybe you're right, maybe we both have our reasons, so you could say that our needs meet neatly in the centre.' He lowered his head and outlined her mouth with his tongue. She didn't respond but neither did she draw back. 'Let go, Sara. We make good sex—no, we make magnificent sex. Why not?' He pushed himself away and she realised that she had been holding her breath. 'Think about it. I'll be gone by the time you get back with Simon.' He paused at the door to give her a brief nod. 'I'll be in touch.'

The barracuda circling its prey. Sara closed her eyes briefly and, once she had heard the slam of the kitchen door, wearily headed down the stairs.

CHAPTER SIX

IT WAS raining outside. Nothing spectacular, just an incessant fine drizzle that turned the London streets into slippery grey grime. James pushed himself away from his desk and swivelled his chair round so that he was staring out into the darkening skies. An uninspiring view, but even if he went to the massive glass windows and looked down the view would be equally uninspiring. By now, most of the nine-to-fivers would have already left work and the pavements would be relatively deserted. The City, with its monuments to financial success, thronged with people during the day but by night it was comparatively quiet. Only the diehards would be still at work at a little after nine at night.

Diehard workaholics, he thought grimly, and me. Two weeks ago he would have classified himself as one of those workaholics, but in the space of a fortnight his ability to function seemed to have taken a knocking. Several times he had found himself staring at the rows of figures on his computer only to realise after a few minutes that he had actually not been taking anything in at all.

Like tonight. Friday night. He would normally have reviewed all the details of this latest merger by now and would be getting geared up to go out, maybe to a restaurant or one of the more low-key, members-only jazz clubs that he favoured, with something delectable, nubile and willing.

But he was only halfway through his review and had already lost interest. As for the delectable, nubile, willing companion…

He clicked his tongue in irritation and began prowling through his spacious office.

The last woman he had taken out four days ago had been an unmitigated disaster. She had seemed quite sexy and vivacious the last time he had met her three months ago at a stunningly dull cocktail party hosted by one of his friends for a foreign ambassador with extensive, useful connections. She had flirted outrageously with him and had been suitably peeved when he had told her that he would, regrettably, not be around to continue their flirting because he was due to fly to New York the following day, and then on to the Far East. He had taken her number and promptly forgotten all about her. Until four days ago, when taking her out had seemed an inspired idea. Delectable, nubile and willing had been just what he needed to combat the daily intrusive images of a tall, slender red-haired witch who had sent him packing and in the process left him nursing emotions that were driving him crazy.

Unfortunately, Annabel had failed to achieve what he had hoped she would. Her short, tight, sequinned dress had screamed garishness, her all-over tan had added to the impression and her conversation had left him bored out of his skull.

Back to the proverbial drawing board, he thought grimly. But he wasn't going to get in touch with Sara. In the cold light of day, his words, casually spoken before he had headed out of the Rectory, had been exposed for what they were. A pathetic play for a woman who had made it clear in no uncertain terms that she might have slept with him once, but beyond that she was going nowhere. At least she had been honest enough not to fall back on the tired excuse about having had too much to drink, but he couldn't stop the nagging, unpleasant suspicion that several glasses of wine had played a bigger part than he cared to admit.

He was so absorbed in frowning contemplation that it took a few seconds for the sound of the telephone to connect with his brain, then for his hand to connect with the receiver.

The minute he heard her voice, he froze before slowly turning around so that he could perch on the edge of his desk and look outside at the darkening sky.

'And to what do I owe the pleasure of this call?' His voice was cold, uninviting.

Hundreds of miles away, Sara heard it without the slightest tremor of apprehension.

'I'm so glad I got through. I thought perhaps you might have gone out as it's Friday night.'

Which only reminded him why precisely he hadn't gone out. His lips thinned with angry self-disgust.

'Cut the pleasantries, Sara, and get to the point. Why have you called and what do you want?'

Get to the point? Sara nearly laughed. Oh, yes, she'd get to the point, all right, in her own sweet time.

'And thank you so much for asking how I am, James. As well as can be expected, now that you don't mention it.'

'How did you get hold of my mobile number?'

'Oh, I asked your mother. I told her that Simon wanted something from Harrods and I wanted you to see whether you could bring it up for him the next time you came.'

'And I am supposed to what…? In response to that? Feel a sudden surge of curiosity? Admire you for your inventiveness? Just say what you have to say and get off this line. I'm on my way out and I don't have time to stand here having a conversation with you.' In which case, he thought cynically, why do I not simply hang up? Rage and frustration washed over him and he found that he was still gripping the receiver.

'I don't expect admiration for my inventiveness, but the surge of curiosity might be nice. I phoned because I wanted to hear your voice, because I want to see you, James.'

'You want to see me. Would that be so that we can have a re-run of our last conversation? You *do* remember our last conversation, don't you? The one when you told me to leave?' He found that he was prowling the office with the phone, like an animal in a cage. He even felt like an animal, awash with primitive feelings that he couldn't seem to decipher.

'I remember it. I've thought about it. I've done nothing *but* think about it...' Not quite true. She had had one or two other things on her mind very well. Just as well he couldn't see into her mind, just as well he couldn't see what was really going on inside her, underneath the controlled, smoky voice with just the right mixture of apology, seriousness and invitation.

But God, it hurt to hear him. Hurt in every pore of her body, in places she never even knew existed. And to think she had once considered Phillip the only man capable of delivering pain! What he had delivered had been a bouquet of flowers in comparison.

'I've spent hours just remembering, James. The way we laughed together, the way you made me feel...' The way you used me.

The bitter memory of her conversation with Lucy Campbell rose up inside her mind like a monster.

'So,' the small blonde had drawled with a malicious little smile playing on her lovely mouth, 'I hear you and James Dalgleish can't keep your hands off one another...'

Sara had bumped into her purely by accident the day

before and, from the position of not knowing her from Adam, was rapidly made aware of precisely who she was, how long she had known the Dalgleish family, and where her ambitions lay. Very definitely in the direction of sex, marriage and babies.

'Then your source of information needs to brush up on her spying skills.' But Sara flushed guiltily at the memory of them in bed together, making love with fierce, explosive urgency. She had done what she had needed to do, but all she could do was remember. He was still with her.

'Really?' Lucy's mouth curved into a well-bred smile of amusement. 'I shouldn't bother getting my hopes up if I were you,' she mused thoughtfully. 'James is not open to being caught, especially by *you*.'

'I'm not trying to catch anyone...'

'I don't suppose he told you...' One fine eyebrow was arched speculatively. 'No...of course he wouldn't have. No one can say that he isn't clever...'

'Told me what?'

'Why he's taking such an interest in you. Good heavens, James could have his pick of any woman, anywhere. So...why you?'

'I don't have to listen to this.'

'No, you don't, but...' Lucy shrugged with just the right amount of insolent indifference to forestall Sara's decision to walk away. 'I would if I were you. In fact, you'll probably thank me afterwards...'

'I doubt that.' But still she wavered.

'Oh, I wouldn't bank on it. For someone who's supposed to be smart, and believe me I've already heard all about your big, powerful job in London, you're incredibly trusting. I mean, do you really imagine that James Dalgleish, a man who could have literally *anyone*, would be interested in *you* if there wasn't a motive?'

'Motive? What are you talking about?'

'The Rectory, of course. Hasn't he mentioned it to you? That he wants to get his hands on your house? Has wanted that place for years? I must say, darling, that I have to take my hat off to him. What better way to get what he wants than to sleep with the woman who owns it? So much easier to persuade someone to do what you want them to do when you're lovers, wouldn't you say?' She looked at Sara with a smirk. 'See? Now, haven't I done you a favour?'

Sara dragged herself back to the present and the task that lay before her.

Revenge.

And why not? Why the hell not? She had been used and she wasn't going to slink away and lick her wounds in private. Phillip had been a disaster, but James...

Her stomach clenched at the devastation he had managed to wreak. And he had managed it because she had been a fool, simple as that. She had allowed herself to trust, to feel, to open up to him and he had played on her trust to get a little closer to what he had wanted. And it had not been her.

She found that her fingers were white, clenched around the telephone cord, her nails biting into the soft flesh of her palm. She forced herself to relax. But it was so hard, because even now, knowing it all, knowing him for the kind of man he was, that deep, sexy voice was still managing to pierce through her like a knife.

'Haven't *you* thought about us at all?'

'A trip down memory lane, Sara?' But dammit, yes, he remembered. All too clearly.

'I haven't slept since you left, James...' And she hadn't. She hadn't slept, functioned, barely eaten. She had been in pain. And then when she had met Lucy, had realised what was going on, she still hadn't slept, and the pain was

still there, the pain of knowing that she had been manip-
ulated by a man she had finally seen as a far cry from
Phillip.

'This is a pointless conversation.' But still he couldn't
replace the receiver and he could hear a husky shakiness
in his voice that made him want to hurl something very
heavy straight through the window.

'Remember how good we were in bed? You said so
yourself and you were right. We made love and it was
never like that for me. Never.' The truth of that ac-
knowledgment made her eyes hurt with unshed tears. She
drew in her breath and continued speaking but her voice
was wobbly. 'The way you touched me...the places that
you touched...I felt alive. When you kissed me, I felt as
though I was on fire...and then when you kissed other
parts of me, James...my breasts, my nipples, my stomach...'

'Just good sex. I believe that was the conclusion you
arrived at.' He was having difficulty thinking clearly. Her
words were evocative and her voice filled his head like
incense.

'And I thought that good sex was not a reason for carrying on with a relationship...' Images of him assaulted
every corner of her mind.

Good sex. A meeting of two bodies, but lord, so much
more than that. For her.

She had sent him on his way, yes, and he had suppos-
edly walked out of her life two weeks ago, but she could
see now, through her anguish and disillusionment, that he
would have re-entered it soon enough. He was a clever
and experienced man and one with a mission. He would
simply have banked on her attraction to him to railroad
through her defences. And then when the time was right,
he would have begun talking to her about the Rectory,

allowing his ability to make love to overcome her questions.

Just you remember that, Sara told herself bitterly.

'I'm here in London for a couple of days,' she said, scenting her words with promise. 'I have to sort out arrangements with my flat. Routine stuff. I really would love to meet up with you. I'm staying in a hotel in Kensington, actually, so I'm quite central...and we could talk...'

'And you think I should make time for you?'

'Yes, yes, I do. I dented your ego the last time we met and I would like to make up for that...' She very nearly said that she had hurt him, but of course he wouldn't have been hurt by her rejection. Just temporarily frustrated until he felt the time was right to pounce again.

'Oh, really? And how do you intend to *make up for that*?' A dented ego was something he could deal with. He mentally began a process of damage limitation by telling himself that that was really all there was to it. That the hurt and anger he had felt was just a reflection of a man accustomed to having everything being denied something.

'I would very much like to buy you dinner. You name the restaurant. I'm here on my own, so there'll be no need for me to rush back to my room...' She purposefully dropped her voice a couple of notches lower. 'Not that it's that much of a room, to be honest. Just a dressing table and a chest of drawers and a bathroom and, of course, a bed...'

Was she doing this on purpose? James thought, stifling his sudden urge to groan. He had not seen her as an out-and-out flirt before but either she was genuinely naïve in not knowing that a few choice words could send a man's pulses rocketing, or else she was blatantly offering him...herself...and the thought of that turned him on as nothing on this green planet ever had in his life before.

'I was going to bring Simon with me,' she was saying, although he was only dimly aware of her voice because his mind had taken off on a tangent and he seemed incapable of reining it back in, 'but your mum said that she would love nothing better than to have him stay with her. I don't know if she told you, but he's been over there a couple of times…to play with the train set. He's never had a train set of his own; it just wasn't possible in the flat in London. Anyway, I would like to see you, James. Of course, if you don't have time…'

He would have time though. She was sure of it. With a cynicism she had not thought herself capable of, she reflected that he still wanted the Rectory. The bait was dangling very close to him. She was sure he would grab it, but just in case…

'I think it makes sense, though, don't you, James? We should be on speaking terms, considering we'll probably bump into one another whenever you happen to be in Scotland. It's a small place and if tongues wagged when we had that one silly kiss…' she laughed throatily '…well, they'll be wagging even more if you show up and insist on walking past me on the street without saying a word…'

The lifeline of cold rationality rescued him from his warring pride.

He relaxed fractionally and moved to sit back down in his swivel chair.

'So we meet up and discuss…what? Politics? The weather? World poverty?'

'We meet up and discuss what a fool I was…' Sara allowed herself to pause while her mind raced ahead to her own conclusions, that she had indeed been a fool—to have involved herself with him in the first place '…to think that I could say goodbye to you and walk away unscathed…' Truth was cleverly intermingled with lies. She would never have imagined in a thousand years that she would be capable of a cold-blooded game of revenge, but there was a knife twisting in her gut that made it much easier than she might have thought possible.

He still wanted her house. He would come. And she would sleep with him because she enjoyed it. She would take what he had to offer her instead of squeezing shut her legs and talking about principles, and when she was finished she would dump him, but not until she had informed him in no uncertain terms that she had known from the word go what game he had been playing and thanks for the good time but the house was staying in her possession.

'Also,' Sara murmured convincingly, 'Simon is fond of your mother. If you decide that you want to have nothing to do with me, then it might be awkward for them both...'

'Well, why not?' James drawled. He had a dinner engagement the following night with a client, but it wouldn't be a problem to either defer that or else let Ray Cooper cover for him. 'If keeping up appearances means that much to you.' His voice was lazy, bored, indifferent, but he couldn't help himself from feeling a certain brooding excitement at the thought of seeing her again. An irresistible weakness.

'Where would you like to go?'

'I can't say that I really care one way or the other and I haven't got time now to debate such an irrelevance. As I said, I'm on my way out.'

'In which case, I know an excellent Italian restaurant. La Taverna...' Overplaying her case at this point wouldn't be a good idea. He was a man of formidable pride and she had dented it. She didn't need him to walk away from her invitation.

'Right.'

'It's in Chelsea. Just off the King's Road as a matter of fact. Quite informal.'

'Right. I'll be there at seven-thirty, even though this charade leaves me cold.'

'Seven-thirty.' Sara filled her voice with bubbling pleasure. 'Can't wait, James…'

She spent the following day in a state of barely suppressed excitement underlined with grim determination to see this plan through.

She had arranged to meet three of her friends for lunch, had envisaged a fun, gossipy and bonding couple of hours with them but was bitterly disappointed. Her mind was too full of what lay ahead in a few hours' time and she had moved away from ribald tales of office politics, promotions in the offing and prospective bonuses.

Had this been what it had been all about for her as well? The feverish plans to make even more money? The restricted lunch breaks and long working hours so that she could afford the nanny and the mortgage and the lifestyle that she had usually been too exhausted to appreciate?

It niggled at the back of her mind and she realised, with another familiar spurt of pain, that these were the very things she would have wanted to talk to James about. She would have enjoyed nothing more than to sound him out about what she was feeling.

And she would have done—a lifetime ago.

Now, though…

She got dressed very slowly for an evening seducing the enemy.

She was wearing a short cream silk skirt that floated sexily around her thighs and exposed her long legs to the absolute maximum. A figure-hugging cream top with sleeves to the elbows that just hit her waistline, leaving a tantalising glimpse of skin whenever she moved. High

shoes that emphasised her height. Hair loosely curling
down her back.

Half of her hoped that he would already be at the restaurant, waiting for her, so that he could be afforded the
full impact of her walking slowly towards him. The other
half hoped that she would be the first to arrive so that she
could have a little time to get her thoughts together before
she laid eyes on him.

Plan or no plan, she wasn't a complete idiot.

She knew that just seeing him for the first time in two
weeks was going to have an effect on her. She might be
bitterly hurt at his treatment, and that alone would be
enough to give her the courage she needed to do what she
wanted to do. But she would also have his disturbing sexuality to contend with as well. She would have to with-
stand those amazing eyes on her face, hear that voice that
could send electric currents racing along her spine, watch
the sensuous curve of his mouth.

He was there by the time she arrived, waiting for her.

Sara saw him as soon as she walked into the restaurant.
Indolently lounging on his chair right at the back, cradling
a drink in his hand.

God, but he looked right at home here. Swarthy, black-
haired, so ferociously good-looking that she gave a small
gasp. She couldn't help it.

She wanted his eyes to travel the length of her, but as
she walked towards him she still felt horribly and acutely
self-conscious.

Fortunately it didn't show in her voice when she finally
made it to the table and was standing looking down at him.

'Haven't been waiting long, have you?' She smiled.
Panic, misery and a certain amount of treacherous elation
rushed through her. She took her time to sit down. 'I would
have got here a little sooner, but the traffic was absolutely

foul. It's so easy to forget how mad things are down here compared to Scotland, isn't it?'

'What are you drinking?'

If he was trying to imply uninterest, then he was succeeding. Sara leaned forward, elbows on the table, and smiled at him. No response.

'Wine, I think. What have you got there?'

'Whisky.' He swallowed a mouthful and continued to look at her coldly.

'Shall we share a bottle of white wine? I need something cold. It's so warm out there. I can't remember a summer like this in years.'

'Ah, the weather.' His mouth curled into a humourless smile. 'Favourite standby of people struggling for conversation.' He leaned forward and Sara felt the full force of his masculinity like a physical blow.

'I'm not struggling for conversation, James, I'm attempting to make some.' The waiter came and there was temporary relief from the effect he was having on her as he scanned the wine list and ordered a bottle of Chablis.

'And who am I to thwart your efforts? So, the weather. Is it still sunny in Scotland? Or have there been a few showers?'

'Don't.'

'Don't what?'

'Be facetious.'

'You forget, this was your splendid idea. To meet up so that we could chat like two sensible adults and smooth the path for a workable relationship should we ever happen to meet when I'm next up there.'

'What have you been doing since we last…saw one another?'

'Have we finished with the weather?'

The wine arrived, was poured, and Sara drank most of her glass in the space of a few seconds.

Where was all the charm? she thought acidly. Now that his plans had been scuppered, did he not see any further point in trying to expend any on her?

'I've finally been meeting a few people.' She twirled the wine glass in one hand and propped her chin in the palm of the other. 'Fiona has been wonderful. Asking us over for tea, introducing Simon to some of the other children, introducing me to some of her friends. I just wish I could have been able to get into it a little bit more…'

'At which point,' he leaned forward as well so that the distance between them was narrowed to the point where giddiness took over, 'I expect I am to ask you what you mean by that remark…'

'What's the point making things difficult between us?'

'You need to ask that question?'

This was how he had done it, of course. That way he had of focusing absolutely and entirely on her. Even now, when every pore of him breathed hostility, he could still make her feel sick with self-awareness. He had a male aggression that made Phillip seem like a boy in comparison.

'We're adults. Adults make mistakes. I've already confessed to making one, to turning you away…'

'Something no woman has ever done.' He knew how he sounded. Bloody petulant. He could have kicked himself but the words were out before he could retract them.

'And I've never had a one-night stand in my life.' She watched, gratefully, as the waiter poured her another glass of wine and was aware of them ordering food, but only just. 'Have you missed me?'

James felt himself flush darkly. 'I think I prefer conversing about the weather,' he drawled, noticing the deli-

cate flush that invaded her cheeks at his response. 'As to
what I have been doing...' He sat back, giving himself
some breathing space. The directness of her question had
rattled him. If he had tried to answer that one, he was
certain that she would have been able to glean the truth
from his expression. 'Working.'

'All work and no play...'

'Makes James a dull boy?' They were making short
work of this wine, he thought and he was nettled by the
admission to himself that he felt as if he needed it. What
the hell was he doing here?

'Hardly dull, from what I remember...'

'How is my mother?' he asked heavily. He had ordered
some kind of fish, which appeared to have now been
placed in front of him and looked delicious, although the
consumption of food was the last thing on his mind.

'Fine. Enjoying the weather and the gardens, you
know...'

'And Simon?' It was a struggle to keep the conversation
low-key and normal but he had to. He had to stay in control because, against every sensible bone in his body, he
was responding to her, to whatever dance she was leading
him, and it enraged him.

'Simon is fine. He...he really enjoys living up there. Of
course, I've told him that the weather helps and that it's
completely different in winter, with the cold and the snow,
but that just seems to get him more excited. Would you
believe he's never seen snow?' Sara began eating. Instead
of being coolly in control, she felt flustered and vulnerable.
She had to remind herself why she was here, why she was
having dinner with this man...

'No, London never gets snow, does it?' He gave a short,
derisive laugh. 'And now we are back to the weather.'

No, we're not, Sara thought fiercely. We are *not* going

to run around in circles, getting nowhere. I am *not* going to abort my plan and let you get away with using me. I won't be hurt by you and allow myself to run away.

It was so tempting to ask him *why*, to ask him whether he had felt anything for her at all, that she had to lower her eyes and take a few deep, steadying breaths.

'So we are. Silly, isn't it? When there's so much else to talk about.'

'For instance?'

'For instance I could tell you that you look good, that I'd forgotten just how good you look.' She quietly closed her knife and fork, leaving her food unfinished, and met his eyes steadily.

'What are you playing at?' He pushed his plate away, deposited his napkin on it and sat back, staring at her, willing himself to get a grip, knowing that nothing was showing on his face but that his bloody nervous system was in a state of chaos.

'I'm talking.'

'Talking.'

'That's right. That's why I got in touch with you. So that we could have a conversation, although…'

'Although what…?' he asked, his words dropping softly into the silence between them.

'Although I can think of much more interesting things to do…'

CHAPTER SEVEN

'OH, REALLY?'

'Really. To be perfectly honest, I could have handled everything with my banker and the estate agents by phone or e-mail. There was no real need to travel down here to London, but…' Those intent blue eyes could make a girl think she was drowning, Sara thought.

'But you just couldn't resist the desire to feast your eyes on my magnificent self.'

'No, that isn't all there is to it. And it's rude to draw attention to yourself like that. Makes you sound egotistic. Which, of course, you are.'

James glanced away but she could see that he wanted to smile and that little glimpse of humour made her heart contract.

'So I am rude, egotistic…I cannot imagine why you would make a trip to London to communicate with someone with those personality traits.'

'I really did want to talk to you, James. I really did think that it would have been crazy to just cease communication completely when we're going to inevitably keep bumping into one another. And you may be rude and egotistic but you're also interesting and fairly amusing.'

'Fairly amusing. Well, we're stepping up the ladder of compliments. Now that you've had your way telling me what you think of me, I feel it's only right that I tell you what I think of you…'

A little shiver of apprehension raced down her spine. She didn't want him to tell her anything of the sort. She just didn't need any more of his lies, any more pretence that he was interested enough in her to have formed opinions of her at all.

'You look alarmed,' he murmured, letting his eyes wander away from hers, to her mouth, to her breasts. 'I think you're immensely complex and a complete mystery. One minute you're lecturing to me like a minister on a pulpit, the next minute you're flirting with me and inviting me back into your bed. Now, that makes no sense, does it?'

'Does it have to?' Sara laughed and tossed her head. She had never tossed her head in her life before and was surprised that the gesture seemed to come so naturally. 'Women are allowed to be unpredictable, aren't they?' She rested her head on her hand and gazed at him with a half-smile.

Unbelievably, she was enjoying this.

'I thought men loved unpredictability in women. Besides, if I'm mysterious and complex, then I must also be unpredictable. They go hand in hand.'

'Not all men love unpredictability.' He didn't. It appeared, though, that she was the exception because the way she was looking at him now was making his senses reel and it was all he could do to keep his hands in check.

'You mean *you* don't?'

'I mean I should get the bill and…'

'And…?'

She could sense the wary restlessness in him and on the spur of the moment she reached out her hand and covered his, very, very lightly and very, very briefly, just long enough to stroke the side of his thumb with her finger. Then her hand was back in place and burning. His power over her could threaten everything, but she wouldn't let it.

'You're skating on thin ice, Sara.' He raked his fingers

through his hair, but his eyes never left her face, not for one single second.

'Care to explain?'

'What if I decide to take you up on your very generous offer? Are you really going to feel any differently about me if we sleep together again? And again after that? Am I not still going to be the big, bad wolf who should keep away from your door?'

'It's all a question of choices, isn't it?'

'Choices?'

'I can choose to foresee the difficulties and walk away before they arise, or I can choose to run headlong into whatever lies ahead and realise that experience, whatever the outcome, counts for a lot.' Too much talk and too much truth. She smiled seductively. Another little talent she didn't know she possessed. Whatever this man brought out in her, he was unique. 'I choose the latter.'

Who the hell was he to talk about skating on thin ice when he could barely think straight with those feline eyes looking at him?

The circular table separating them was small bordering on tiny and he had to fight the temptation to slouch slightly further down into his chair, just far enough so that he could insert his thigh underneath that very short, very sexy skirt of hers. Feel the softness of her crotch against the hardness of his knee. God, he wanted her.

'I don't think this is the place to have a prolonged conversation, though...' She was unaware that the lowering of her eyelids and the flick of her tongue over her lips was as erotic as a striptease.

'Where,' he heard himself saying, 'do you have in mind, in that case...?'

Sara shrugged and looked down as she casually traced the rim of her glass with one finger. 'Any suggestions?'

Several, he knew he should say, *and all involve two minutes on the end of a phone while you're heading back up to Scotland and I'm here, working, going out with women I can predict and getting on with life before you came along and managed to clutter it up.* He was as cynical as they came! Jaded from experience and permanently watchful of the dangers of losing his massive self-control.

He signalled to a waiter for the bill.

Sara could see the questions racing through that clever brain of his. But his questions didn't matter. He was going to pay the bill, no dessert, no coffees, no chatting over liqueurs, and that could only mean one thing. He was going to come with her. She felt a kick of satisfaction and, hard on the heels of that, a rush of undiluted, naked longing.

This was going to be a learning curve for her, she thought a little wildly. She couldn't go through life choosing men who thought nothing of pulling the rug out from under her feet. She would toughen up and if it was at his expense then that was just too bad. He deserved everything he got.

Knowing what she now knew, she should have been left cold by him, but the minute she had laid eyes on him she had felt her body begin to react, and as he paid the bill, ignoring her insistence on paying half, she felt the lick of excitement steadily getting stronger.

The silence between them was electric. As was the fact that he didn't touch her. Once outside the restaurant, he shoved his hands in his pockets, only withdrawing one to hail a black cab. He leaned down, gave the driver an address in Chelsea, and once they were both inside he sprawled against his side of the car so that he could look at her.

'So, are you going to tell me what brought about this change of heart?'

'I already told you,' Sara said, taking quick breaths, 'I thought things over and, well…you were right. It's crazy to go through life being affected by what Phillip did. We're adults and we were…' She sighed with remembered pleasure and that sigh had nothing to do with revenge or bitterness.

'Good together in bed? Fantastic, in fact?'

Sara raised her eyebrows in unexpected amusement. 'I think I can hear your ego again.'

'Tut, tut. Now, that's not very nice considering you're the seductress trying to woo me back between the sheets, is it?' His deep, velvety voice caught her amusement and shared it. It gave her an uneasy premonition of how simple it would be to fall right back into the trap of opening up to him, because on a very basic level she just seemed to click with him.

'I've never been called a seductress before.' Uneasy premonitions didn't have a part to play.

'Mm. I can understand why. Brutal honesty isn't usually the mark of the seductress.'

His voice was wickedly smooth and she dared to extend her hand so that it was resting lightly on his thigh.

'Blame my job,' Sara murmured, her pulses leaping at the casual physical contact. 'Being brutally honest becomes a habit after a while. Does it scare you?' She moved her hand fractionally higher and was almost disappointed when he covered it firmly with his own before she could take her explorations further.

'Oh, I don't scare easily. Not,' he added in a drawl, 'that you won't have to use other feminine wiles to tempt me…'

'Other feminine wiles such as what…?' Was this really

her talking? Flirting outrageously and loving every minute of it? Good lord.

His response to that was to remove his hand from where it had been covering hers. Sara thought that if she listened hard enough she might just be able to hear the wild beat of her heart and the leap of her pulses as she edged her hand higher until it lay over the hard rod of his erection, which she could feel throbbing beneath the fabric of his trousers.

He shifted slightly. 'Now, if I'd had my driver I might just have asked you to take your technique a little further.' He could almost smell the musky aroma of her excitement, filling his nostrils and making him want to unzip his trousers and push her hand harder against him.

'But regrettably,' he said roughly, 'no driver and we're just about here at my apartment.' On cue, the taxi slowed down and Sara's pulse rate returned to something approaching normality as she slipped out of the cab and watched with her arms folded across her as he paid the fare and then turned to look at her.

'This time,' he murmured, walking up to her and positioning himself directly in front of her with his legs slightly parted, 'no turning back. If you think you're going to suffer with agonies of conscience afterwards, or even before for that matter, then you can leave in the next cab. This isn't going to be a one-night stand.'

'You mean you want an affair.'

'If you want to call it that.'

'What else can we call it?'

'We can call it whatever we want to,' he informed her silkily, 'after all, it's just a matter of vocabulary. But we both know what we're talking about.'

'What about a relationship, then?' Sara threw at him. She knew that he wouldn't like the idea of that, for all his talk about it just being *a matter of vocabulary*. An affair was something frothy and light that dissolved in a puff of wind, but a relationship was something more than that and, considering that he had his own hidden agenda for sleeping with her, then going beyond a bit of froth would not be something he would even contemplate for a minute. Oh, no, that would be just a little too much like hard work for him.

'I don't have a problem with that,' he surprised her by saying. In the dim pool of light reflected from the nearest street lamp, he could see her startled expression. She wasn't interested in a relationship, he thought. Never mind what she said about moving away from her past, she was still as trapped in it as she ever was. He felt a sudden, searing determination to snap her out of it, focus her entirely on him, as a lover and as a man as well.

'Feeling a little scared at the thought of getting to know me, Sara?' he murmured mockingly and she tilted her chin up defensively.

'Not at all,' she lied.

'Good, so shall we go up to my apartment? I don't know about you, but it's a little too chilly to stand out here debating points of detail.'

The building was severe and imposing from the outside. The white façade was broken by intricate black wrought-iron railings around the long windows, and apart from a few window-boxes there was a total absence of green. It was as different from his mansion in Scotland as it was possible to get. Somehow it summarised the life in London that had woven such a magical spell over her when she had left it behind, but which, now that she was in it once more even if only for a couple of days, was already beginning to impinge uncomfortably on her.

Two of the four-storeyed buildings had obviously been

cleverly knocked into one so that the reception area was not a small hallway, leading up to a single staircase, but a large central area, impeccably tiled, and at one end there was a small walnut desk manned by a uniformed middle-aged man who half stood when James walked in.

'I thought you'd given up the night shift,' James said, grinning as he collected his mail.

'I had, sir.' The weathered face returned the grin. 'But then I discovered that it beats being at home with the wife, the mother-in-law, the daughter and the little nipper. Soon as the mother-in-law goes back to Oz and Gary finishes the house repairs so that Ellie and little Tommy can move in, then I'll take back up my day post. Be able to watch a little night-time telly in peace and quiet.'

'And I guess you spend all day sleeping?' James raised his eyebrows and tapped the wad of post against the open palm of one hand.

'Not *all*, sir. There's a limit to what the wife will tolerate.'

James was still grinning as the elevator door purred shut on them. 'He's an institution here,' he explained with a devastating smile. 'Been here as long as I have.'

'Which is how long, exactly?' Sara asked curiously.

'Almost six years. Before that I had a mews house in Richmond but this is a helluva lot more convenient for central London.'

'And no troublesome garden to take care of.'

'And no troublesome garden to take care of,' he agreed, standing back to allow her to exit first. 'I presume that was your reason for an apartment as well?'

'Yes,' she admitted, 'although with a child, a garden would have been ideal. But I just would never have had the time to look after it and it would have been too small in central London, anyway, to employ the use of a gardener.'

'So you went from one extreme to the other.'

'Simon adores it.' She shrugged, watching him as he smoothly unlocked his door and pushed it open, automatically turning to deactivate his alarm.

'And you?'

Sara pretended to ignore the question. It wasn't difficult. He had switched on the light and she was quite literally speechless at what she saw. Acres of space. Acres of space for a London apartment at any rate. Shallow stairs led away from the door and down to a superb sunken sitting area which rose on one side to give an open view of yet another sitting area, less formal, with a television set at one end and alongside that a desk with a complex array of office equipment. On the other side, the sunken area led up to a spacious dining area and beyond that the kitchen, which was, unheard of in a London flat, large enough to house a kitchen table as well as all the usual culinary paraphernalia. A long counter, topped with black granite, separated the kitchen from the dining area, but aside from that one division the eye could travel the width of the room without being obstructed by any doors. And the gleaming wooden flooring emphasised the illusion of vast space.

Stretching behind were the doors that led to the bedrooms and bathrooms. It was elegant but understated, as only truly very expensive places were. The paintings on the walls were small, discreet and vaguely familiar.

'And I thought that my apartment was luxurious,' she commented drily, stepping tentatively down the stairs to the sitting area and looking around her slowly.

'Something to drink?' Which reminded her of the reason she was here in the first place, and an unexpected flutter of nerves rippled up to the surface.

'Please.'

'Coffee? Tea?'

'A glass of wine, if you have it.' She followed him up to the kitchen and perched awkwardly on one of the softly padded chairs by the table. 'It's an amazing place,' she said, watching as he poured her a glass of wine and one for himself, before sitting opposite her at the table. Her eyes skittered away from the aggressive planes of his face and the only thing running through her head was the fact that she needed to keep talking. She was no longer the seductress out to even scores. She just felt like a nervous, timid young girl out on her first date with a man who was light-years ahead of her in the sophistication stakes.

'How on earth did you find it? A place like this is like gold dust in London. You must have spent months, years searching.'

'I own the building, actually.' James watched the changing expressions on her face with amusement. 'Or, rather, it's been in the family for as long as I can remember. We used to own quite a bit more as a matter of fact but a lot's been sold along the way to help cover the costs of running the estate in Scotland.'

'Oh, indeed. Don't we *all* have to flog a few of our London assets so that we can keep our country estates running?'

He grinned at the sarcasm, which Sara half wished he hadn't done because she then became all too uncomfortably aware that, manipulator or not, the man had bags of charm, too much for his own good.

'Where were you before you lived in London?' she asked hurriedly.

'Oh, a bit of here and a bit of there.' Those amazing eyes! They would have held her captive if she wasn't so intent on avoiding them. 'Building up my businesses, handling my father's investments. I liked the idea of being fairly rootless.'

'I thought you still were…fairly rootless.'

'I have this place,' he made an expansive gesture to encompass the apartment, 'and Scotland. I'm as rooted as it's possible for any man to be.'

'Not many men own properties all over the globe,' Sara pointed out.

'I consider myself very fortunate in that respect.'

Sara toyed with the stem of her wine glass.

'I'm surprised you haven't been snapped up by now.' She wanted desperately to remember how she was going into this, with her eyes wide open and cold-bloodedly aware that hers was a game without emotion. She didn't want to succumb to any phoney charm. She'd already gone down that road. 'Eligible playboys are always the first to go.'

'That's been your experience, has it?' The lazy smile dropped from his face. 'And I'm not a playboy. In fact, the very description is an insult. Playboys travel from party to party, spending Daddy's money and chasing pretty young things.'

'And you don't chase pretty young things?' She gestured around her. 'This isn't *Daddy's*? You don't party with the best of them?' She dared him to contradict her, to put her back in the angry frame of mind she needed to keep her perspectives within sight.

He looked at her carefully, as if he was making up his mind about something, then he smiled.

'Actually the building belongs jointly to my mother and me now, not that she ever gets the chance to come down to London except for Ascot and Christmas shopping. Sometimes it's odd to think that she was once a model jet setting all over the world.'

Sara was well and truly deflected. 'Didn't she miss...all of this?'

'Oh, she took a little while to settle, she once told me. She missed the shops and the hectic travel and the buzz, but then after a few months she found herself being drawn in to village life. And, of course, she adored the old man. Apparently, she returned to London a few months after she had moved up and found that a lot of her friends were not quite the exciting young things she thought they were.'

A bit like me, Sara thought bitterly, except the only male who stood any chance of holding back her return was five years old. The friends aspect she could understand. *They* hadn't changed, it was *her* lifestyle that had altered. But as for being drawn into village life, she couldn't see it happening. She still had one foot up north, one down south and no one to help her make her mind up.

'How are you finding life in the Highlands?' he asked curiously and immediately her antennae were up. This would be his first step, she thought. He would never come right out with his plan to buy the house from under her feet. He would gently but relentlessly move in and use whatever was necessary to get what he wanted.

'Different.' Sara stood up and stretched. 'Do you mind if I remove my jacket?' Without giving him time to answer, she pulled off the short cream jacket, which left her only in her tight top that fell neatly to the waistband of the skirt.

'Not going to carry on? Shame.' His hooded blue eyes lingered on her. 'I like the thought of my woman doing a striptease in my kitchen.'

His woman. Sara felt a shiver of pleasure at the possessive terminology. Possessive but frankly meaningless. The only thing that really got to this man when it came to women was sex. And she wanted to get to him, didn't she?

She pulled the top over her head and dropped it on the table between them. Her fingers had been trembling when she did that, but as his eyes drifted over her breasts pushing against the lacy bra she felt the same rush of power that had surged through her earlier. The silence between them was erotically charged, only broken when he pushed back his chair and hooked one ankle around another so that he could pull it towards him, enabling him to stretch out his legs and continue his lazy, broodingly sexy appraisal of what she was doing.

In that instant it occurred to her that she would never have been able to do what she was doing if she hadn't been genuinely and intensely attracted to him. She wanted to touch him and have him touch her and she would, but in due course, when the build-up had left them both weak with need.

He had tipped his head back so that his eyes appeared drowsily half-closed as he watched her.

Sara unhooked the bra and slowly pulled each strap down, then the lacy piece of not much was off and joining the discarded top on the table.

Her breasts pointed proudly out for his inspection. She heard his swift intake of breath and half smiled.

She shimmied towards him until she was standing right in front of him, then, very slowly and not taking her eyes away from his darkly flushed face, she rid herself of her skirt. She almost wanted to scream out loud with her desperate craving to be touched. When her body did finally make contact with his, she was sure that she would explode into a thousand fragments.

It almost did. It felt as if it would anyway as he dropped his legs from the chair so that he was holding her between them and then flicked aside the crotch of her panties so that he could lean forward and deeply inhale the scent of her dusky womanliness. He filled his nostrils with it and she allowed herself to drown under the weight of mindless sensation as he ruffled the fine hair between her legs, blowing against it, preparing her for the delicate probing of his tongue on the tip of her swollen, sensitised clitoris.

With a muffled groan, Sara clasped the back of his dark head with her hands and arched back, shifting her stance slightly so that she could more easily open herself up to accommodate the dark head there between her legs.

At one point she heard herself pleading with him to stop in a voice that she barely recognised, and when he did draw back she was still shuddering from the impact of his ravaging, intimate kiss.

'Sit on my lap,' he commanded shakily and she obeyed. He tilted her back and then subjected her throbbing breasts to the same oral exploration that he had afforded her most private parts.

He sucked on each nipple, drawing the roused bud into his mouth so that he could tease it with his teeth and his tongue. His moist mouth was connecting to invisible sensory lines within her body, shooting pleasure straight from the tips of her nipples to those parts of her body which could only be appeased when she rubbed them against the rough fabric of his trousers.

If she carried on doing this she knew that she would not be able to stop bringing herself to an uncontrollable climax, and as if sensing this he pulled back from her throbbing breasts and roughly told her that he needed to get out of his clothes *now*.

What he didn't tell her was that he had never felt so wildly, devastatingly out of control before. He could feel himself bulging against his trousers and it physically *hurt*.

It didn't take him long to divest himself of his clothes, practically ripping his shirt off his back, popping a couple of buttons in the process which bounced across the kitchen floor.

This time when their bodies met, flesh against flesh, there was no room for seductive foreplay.

Their bodies were hot and slick and ripe to be melded together as one. He pulled her back onto him, letting her have just the merest build-up as he clasped his big hands on her waist and encouraged her to feel that intensely arousing friction once again as she rubbed herself wantonly and rhythmically against his hardened shaft. This time there were no knickers and no trousers to impede the heated satisfaction of feeling him massive between her thighs, each thrusting movement bringing an incoherent moan from her parted mouth.

Then with an unsteady groan he inserted himself into her, his powerful body shuddering with satisfaction as she began to undulate on top of him, steadily up and down, increasing her tempo so that her beautiful, bountiful breasts bounced just there by his mouth, just there where he could almost catch them. And God, he wanted to taste them again.

As she moved, his hands swept upwards to capture one jiggling breast and he sucked fiercely on the engorged pink nipple.

It was too much. Did she cry out? She didn't know. Her eyes were closed, her head thrown back, the upper part of her torso pushed forward to accommodate his devastating mouth on her breasts, and then she was free falling through space and time, tumbling over the edge and feeling him taking the same electrifying ride that she was on.

Their bodies were locked into one another and Sara felt that first burst of shattering sensation give way to climactic ripples that took her to a series of peaks that had her sagging when she finally came back down to earth.

It felt somehow *right* when he drew her to him and wrapped his arms around her, slowly tracing the line of her spine with his fingers. She was so peaceful that she could very easily have nodded off.

'I hope you're not too tired...' His voice was a low, husky murmur in her ear and she opened her eyes drowsily to find herself staring at his firm jawline and a glimpse of his mouth that told her he was smiling. Her fingers itched to stroke the edge of his mouth and she resolutely kept them still.

'You couldn't...' Her voice was as husky as his and she didn't recognise the sexy laugh as belonging to her when he informed her that she really shouldn't say things that could possibly constitute a challenge to a man like him.

'But this time I think we'll be a bit more conventional and avail ourselves of my king-sized bed.' He kissed the tip of her nose and she straightened to stare down at him, unbothered by her nudity. They walked with their fingers linked out of the fabulous open area towards one of the doors, which opened into an equally impressive master bedroom.

This section of the house was carpeted and plushly so. Her toes squirmed delightedly into the thick pile and he tugged her towards the bed.

This was a big bed for a big man and the linen was uncompromisingly masculine, a mixture of dark greens and vibrant burgundies that would have left a perfect stranger in no doubt as to the sensual nature of their occupant.

And, just in case she was in any doubt herself, he spent the next hour and a half showing her just how sensual he could be. The frantic urgency of their first bout of love-making, when they had been devoured by a consuming need to get to one another, driven by a primitive sexual

craving that had left them spent and breathless, was replaced by a lingering, almost tender and equally fulfilling
exploration of each other's bodies. It was a slow, melodic
dance that took them both to the same dramatic heights,
but via a different route.

Afterwards, with her brain in neutral and her senses
swimming pleasurably in the aftermath of their lovemaking, Sara coiled herself on her side so that they were facing
one another with their bodies lightly touching.

'I should be going back to my hotel,' she murmured
half-heartedly and he stroked some hair away from her
face.

'I can't think why.'

Sara's brain struggled to get a grip of something very
important that was edging there just out of reach.

'I can't stand the thought of your hanging on to your
past, you know.' James's voice was deadly serious and he
found that he was staring down at her with such ferocious
intensity that he forced himself to dilute it with something
like a low laugh.

'I'm not. Not any more.'

'Tell me about him. Tell me what went wrong.'

'Everything went wrong and it's too long a story to tell,
anyway. Long and tedious and unnecessary.'

'We have time.' He found himself driven to glimpse that
part of her life that was capable of making his teeth snap
together in frustrated anger.

'You mean you're not going to suggest that we…
indulge again?' Sara enquired lightly to break the sudden
tension, and the ploy worked. He smiled. Did he know
how much younger he looked when he smiled?

'I'm no longer a teenager,' James said drily, because he
wanted her to talk and sex would wait. He smiled again
and that smile did it. What harm was there in spilling out

a bit of her personal history to him? It wasn't a state secret, for heaven's sake!

So she found herself telling him about her background, about growing up in the East End of London, helping her father with his market stall, a very thriving market stall, but a market stall nevertheless. She was an only child with a quick brain and her parents had lovingly fostered her talent for schoolwork. By the time she was nine she could run the market stall as efficiently as the best of them and she had enjoyed it. She'd learnt to barter, begun to predict trends in what sold and when it sold and why it sold.

'I never realised it was a talent that would get me where I eventually got, but I was good at…well, trading, I suppose…' She sighed and stared mistily into the distance. Once started, she was discovering that the torrent was unstoppable. Phillip had met her at a social occasion when her star was beginning to shine. He had zeroed in on her and, fool that she had been, she had taken him at face value, she was clever but not clever enough to spot the snob behind the charming veneer.

'So I never thought twice about telling him all about my parents, where I had grown up. He was appalled. Not,' she added truthfully, 'that I think that that was the reason it all went pear-shaped. But it certainly didn't help matters. He had no need for bright stars with dubious backgrounds. In fact, as it turned out, he had no need for bright stars at all. He's marrying someone with no pretensions to a career but presumably good breeding stock. Unlike me. The pregnancy was the last straw. He felt guilty to start with, he wasn't a complete monster, but soon he began implying that, since it was my fault, he had no duties to deal with it, with his own son. Every so often he would come around unannounced, I suppose when one of his twinges of guilt got a little hard to handle, but all that stopped after a while.

He hadn't wanted a child and he especially couldn't deal with a son who wasn't the picture of robust health.' Sara sighed and managed a weak smile. 'So there you go.'

'Market trader,' James murmured softly, reaching to place a kiss on her mouth, 'I like it.' And he did. Although if anyone was to ask him precisely why, he would not have been able to provide an adequate answer.

CHAPTER EIGHT

BY THE middle of August, Sara realised that her initial decision to leave Scotland in time to get Simon back to London for school at the beginning of September was no longer on the cards. She had done nothing about arranging somewhere to live, had checked out no schools either in or around London, and whenever she thought about it her mind went unhelpfully blank.

She blamed James. For someone who worked and lived in London, he had certainly found it inside himself to break with his routine so that he could see her, sometimes two or three times during the week, always in the evening when Simon was not around. When he came up on the weekends, all three of them, she insisted that they meet only at night. She said that her days were just too full trying to get the house together and seeing about the million and one things that still needed doing. In fact, she made sure not to be around on the Saturdays she knew he would be travelling up to his estate.

She arranged to explore anywhere and everywhere. She took her shopping trips as far away from home base as she could. She even made a mammoth effort to take Simon across to Edinburgh, giving themselves a little stay-over treat, although all she could think about was the prospect of seeing James when she got back on the Sunday evening.

She adored the way he waited impatiently for her. She could imagine him striding through the millions of rooms in his mansion, frowning with his hands shoved into his pockets, waiting for her phone call informing him that Simon was settled.

'It's ridiculous,' he had ground out the weekend before, when she had calmly informed him that no, she couldn't possibly go out with him during the day. ' I need to be in your company and yet when I come up here you do nothing but insist I keep away.'

Her laughter had managed to coax a reluctant smile from him, but pretty soon she knew that she wouldn't be able to hold him at bay by telling him that those were her rules and she wanted them respected. He had held off so far but he was like a caged tiger, biding his time until he could push further forward.

She also knew that pretty soon she would have to do what she had set out to do—confront him with his own unpleasant little scheme to buy her house and declare herself the winner, show him that she was nobody's fool and that she could play the sex game as competently as he thought he could.

She was sitting in the garden, half reading a book and half keeping an eye on Simon, who was busily digging up some weeds for her in the hope of finding either worms or buried treasure. She rested her head back, closed her eyes for a few seconds, and when she opened them again it was to see James standing in front of the French doors, watching her.

Sara sat up and blinked but the vision refused to disappear. In fact, the vision strode towards her, long, lean and unfairly sexy in his lightweight trousers and short-sleeved shirt that hung over his trousers.

'I thought you had a thousand things to do and weren't going to be around,' he said, finally standing in front of her and staring down at her flushed face.

Simon had stopped his energetic exploration of the flower bed so that he could look at James.

'What are you doing here?'

'You know, you're doing very little for my concentration, lying there in next to nothing.' He smiled very slowly. 'Now, what if some passing stranger had called round and found you dressed like that?'

'Dressed like what?' Sara peered anxiously over to Simon and smiled reassuringly at him. James followed the direction of her gaze to smile at the boy, who grinned back and looked prepared to launch into conversation. Sara thought she'd better nip that in the bud so she told him cheerfully that if he dug a bit deeper she was sure he would find what he was looking for.

'Which is what?' Blue eyes that had the power to scorch refocused on Sara's flushed face.

'Buried treasure or worms. Either is equally acceptable. And you still haven't told me what you're doing here, not,' she added as a postscript, 'that it isn't very nice to see you.' Except not here and not now. She had managed to make very sure that contact with her son was minimal and things weren't going to change there.

Settling scores, which was the object of the exercise or so she kept telling herself, was one thing. She could handle the consequences, but Simon had to be protected from involvement with James.

'I...I thought we had arranged to meet up a bit later...'

'We had but...' James looked up into the cloudless blue sky and squinted. The hot summer agreed with him. Naturally inclined to swarthiness, he had been given by the sun a deep, bronzed colour that made most other people look anaemic in comparison. Especially her, with her ultra-fair skin that needed protecting. Not that he seemed to mind. In fact, she blushed as she remembered some of his more potent adulations of her body.

He glanced back down at her and grinned. 'It was so bloody hot that I couldn't resist driving over to see if I could catch you before you went out. Somehow,' he leaned over, trapping her in her sun lounger, 'Mama, wonderful company though she is, was not quite the woman I fancied spending my Saturday with.'

Sara licked her lips. 'Actually, I was on my way out…'

'In a pair of shorts and a cropped top that barely covers your breasts? Not if I have any say in that.'

'I was going to change first!'

'Out where?'

'Out to the market, actually. I need to buy some vege-tables, food for me to cook for us tonight.'

He hadn't straightened up and the warm suggestiveness of his eyes as they roamed over her face and the upper part of her body made her nipples ache.

'Good,' he murmured, 'I fancy a trip to the market. Always such an adventure, that market of ours. I can drive us there. We can have lunch somewhere.'

'No!'

James frowned and pushed himself up. 'No? Why not?' He narrowed his eyes suspiciously on her face. Sometimes, not very often, he had the disconcerting feeling that the earth, on which his feet were very firmly planted, was shifting ever so slightly under him. This was one of those times. Shouldn't matter a bean, of course, since sex was all there was between them, hot, vibrant, compulsive sex, but he didn't like her immediate rejection of his company.

'Because…then you'd see what I'm buying and the meal tonight wouldn't be a surprise.'

'Let me take you out. You know how much Mama enjoys coming here now to babysit Simon...'

Which was something else, Sara thought guiltily. She hadn't planned it that way, but Simon and Maria seemed to have developed a natural bond and it had been easier to see him away from her own house. More often than not, they went back to his estate and he cooked for her, tempted her palate with delicacies he carried up with him in his helicopter, little morsels of paradise from Fortnum and Mason or Harrods.

Sometimes he would feed her some of the delicious treats, making her recline on one of the sofas in one of the sitting rooms, door firmly closed so that she could stretch out in naked abandonment and nibble what he presented to her. He would kneel by her side, every bit the adoring slave, and then his adoration would become physical, from her toes to the top of her head.

'No, really, James, I'd rather I just went down to the market and got what I need to get.' She reluctantly swung her legs over the side of the sun lounger so that she could make the point. 'And I'll get through it a lot quicker if it's just me and Simon.'

'I have two perfectly functioning legs,' he said tautly, 'I don't think I'll hold you up. If anything, I can help, take Simon for a milkshake, leave you to shop in peace for a couple of hours.'

'No!' Sara said sharply. Her eyes slid across to where her son was busily making an unholy mess of the flowers she had planted only days earlier. Obviously his designated spot had failed to yield the expected treasure. She would have to sort that out later.

'What's the problem, Sara?' OK, so he was being high-handed and obstinate, but he didn't like to think that his

company was surplus to requirements, that she didn't want
him around whenever and wherever she could have him,
because as far as he was concerned that was how it stood
with him at this moment in time. He couldn't stop thinking
about her. It was the most severe case of lust he had ever
experienced. And when they were together she was as
fired-up as he was, so he couldn't understand how she
could draw lines around them the way that she did, the
way she was doing now.

'There *is* no problem.' Their eyes met and she was the
first to look away. 'Come on, Simes, upstairs. You've got
to change. We're going into town to do some shopping.'

'But I haven't found any treasure,' Simon wailed, not
budging.

'What you need is a metal detector,' James said, strolling across and, to Sara's dismay, reaching out one hand to
take his. 'Now, a metal detector will tell you where to find
your buried treasure. It beeps whenever it senses something interesting in the ground.'

Simon was looking a little too enthralled by that for
Sara's comfort, and it was even more alarming when they
both followed her inside the house with Simon willingly
complying with James's brisk assertion that he would
change him so that his mother could get dressed.

'There's no need,' she protested feebly, only to find herself staring into two pairs of implacable eyes.

Of course, James got his way, accompanying them to
the market. This was just what she didn't need, and as
soon as she could she made her feelings absolutely clear.

'This wasn't part of the deal,' she hissed as they ventured into the open-air food market and she could be assured that Simon was distracted enough not to overhear a
word they were saying.

'What *deal*?'

'Me. You. Us. *That* deal.'

Since that was precisely the arrangement he had always enjoyed with every woman he had ever dated, he was surprised to find himself seething with anger at being informed that he was merely part of a deal.

'I don't know that I care for that expression.'

'Why? It's only a *matter of vocabulary*.'

'Ha, ha. What was the real reason for not wanting me tagging along, Sara? Were you planning on meeting someone in town? A man?' He struggled to hide the primitive stab of jealousy underneath a tone of amused cynicism.

Sara stopped to stare at him. 'Don't be ridiculous.'

'Is that what I'm being? You seemed pretty determined not to have me around and don't think I haven't noticed that it's the same on all the weekends I've come up here. You're free for the evening, but inexplicably occupied during the day. Wouldn't you say that that was a little strange? A little *revealing*?'

Sara turned away and gave all her attention to the boy behind the stall and then surprised him by handing over the correct amount of money before he had time to consult his piece of paper, do his sums and tell her how much she owed.

'Well?' James pressed. 'What do you do with yourself during the daylight hours? If there's some man here you've been seeing, I'll…'

'What? Hound him out of town? String him up from the nearest lamppost?'

'Both,' he muttered, scowling, not that he believed that for a minute. He would have heard long before now.

'There's no man. How could I have the energy for anyone else?' she asked truthfully, which went a little way to putting the shadow of a smile back on his face. He took the bags of fruit and vegetables from her.

'We will have lunch together, the three of us,' he stated flatly, and Sara raised her eyebrows at his peremptory tone of voice. 'I know a very pleasant pub about twenty miles away.'

'Twenty miles?'

'No distance at all.' He shrugged and gave her one of those familiar looks that never failed to make her go warm all over. Wicked, arrogant and searingly sexy all wrapped up in one. 'And then I will deliver you and Simon back to the Rectory in one piece and leave you to get on with the absorbing task of cooking for your man.'

'Cooking for my man. Hm. Aren't you just the sort of sensitive, twenty-first-century guy that every liberated woman dreams of finding?' It was so easy to drift into this kind of teasing banter with him and his sense of humour never let her down. He could make her giggle like a teenager. She was practically giggling now as he visibly puffed himself up and looked every inch the sexy caveman, even though he could cook like a dream when he put his mind to it.

'Yes,' he grinned back at her, 'that would be me. The cap certainly fits so, if you don't mind, I think I will wear it. Now, in a *very sensitive* manner, I will take these bags to the car and expect to see you what time…? In about half an hour?'

Sara sighed and gave up. 'OK. A quick lunch and then *you go home* or I shall have your mother swearing at me for hogging you to myself whenever you come up.'

It was only hours later, after an extraordinarily good lunch at a pub in a small village that made their own town seem like a cosmopolitan city in comparison, that Sara took time out to sit down and think. She didn't like where her thoughts went. Somewhere along the line, in that murky place between theory and practice, it had become just too damned comfortable being with James. If he had railed against her for shunning his company during the day, she could have told him that she yearned for him when he wasn't with her. She had managed to hang on to that little piece of maternal protectiveness that made her shy away from encouraging contact between him and her son, but for how much longer?

Today had been something of a revelation. She had watched helplessly as James had bonded with Simon. She was his mum, who made sure that he washed his hands, brushed his teeth, didn't eat too much of the wrong foods, read books with him and did puzzles, but James had talked to him in an amusing man-to-man way that had had Simon's eyes dancing with delight. He had carried him from pub to car on his shoulders, bouncing him up and down until her son had laughed till tears had gathered in his eyes. He had seriously discussed the possibility of do-ing a spot of manly metal detecting together.

Now, as she prepared vegetables, she knew that she would have to do something about the situation.

She would have to break it off, show her hand, but when she thought of doing that, which was frankly what she had set out to do in the first place, her mind baulked.

Realising that she had peeled far too many carrots for two people, she switched to chopping onions, and when her eyes began to water firmly told herself that the onions were to blame.

Cool it down first. That was what she would do. Take her steps carefully because…because…

Because her heart had disobeyed every instruction her

head had given it, she realised with panic. Her heart had boldly opened up and been swept away while all the time she had been kidding herself that she was pulling the strings and being the hard woman she never had been and certainly wasn't now.

The Rectory was a place of seeming orderly control by the time seven-thirty rolled around.

Simon was comfortably tucked up in bed, fast asleep after being read his favourite book for five minutes. The kitchen smelled of garlic and herbs and the fragrant lamb she had spent the afternoon making, even though her mind had been miles away.

She was wearing a straight sleeveless dress, slightly fitted to the waist and then falling softly to mid-calf. Very old-fashioned, especially with her long hair falling in ripples down her back, very Victorian. Very un-sexy. Not an inch of unnecessary leg visible and no part of her body outlined. If she was going to stick to her guns and begin the painful process of phasing him out of her life, then she needed all the help she could get.

Nevertheless, she still felt her resolve wobble by the time the doorbell went and she pulled open the door to find him standing there, with an enormous bouquet of flowers in one hand.

It was the first time he had made any gesture like that and it took her aback. Flowers seemed to imply romance and romance wasn't what he was about.

'From the gardens,' he said roughly, noting her reaction and registering grimly that flowers probably weren't part of the 'deal' either. He thrust them at her and followed her into the kitchen, watching while she floated around, finding a vase, filling it with water, deftly arranging the flowers with an expertise that only his mother seemed to share.

What was she wearing? He hadn't seen her in anything like that dress before, was surprised that she even possessed something as dreamily feminine as that, considering her wardrobe must still bear the imprint of her power outfits. It left an awful lot to the imagination and, on cue, his imagination began to run riot until he had firmly poured cold water over it.

'Hand-picked?'

'What?'

'The flowers. Hand-picked, I presume?'

James shrugged carelessly. 'Not too difficult, considering the profusion of them in the gardens. Smells good in here. Is Simon asleep?'

Sara didn't want to discuss Simon, but mention of his name did remind her that her mission was to bring closure to this peculiar little relationship she and James were having, one which meant relatively little to him she was sure, but which meant far too much to her.

She would never tell him that she had found out about his little plan to use her to get the Rectory. It was humiliating enough now to think about that without bringing it out into the open and besides…she had played a tit-for-tat game that had massively backfired on her. The games were over, the only truth was that she had to get him out of her life because she was so hopelessly embroiled with him now.

'Tell me what's happening in London,' she invited, steering the conversation into neutral waters. 'What's playing at the theatre? Are there any open-air proms happening? I used to go to the open-air proms every year when I was in London. There's nothing quite like listening to good music outside, surrounded by people, with a picnic hamper by your side and friends around you.'

'Any friends in particular?' James took the proffered glass of wine and swallowed a mouthful.

Recently he seemed to have unearthed a distastefully possessive streak that he was finding difficult to control. What friends had she gone there with? He had gone to one open-air prom, last year in fact. He hadn't seen her there then. Who had she been with? Her ex-boyfriend? Some other man? A whole tribe of them?

'Friends from work.' Sara went across to the Aga, opened the door and released a wonderful smell of cooking.

'Do you keep in touch with them still?'

'Of course I do!' She had conversations down the end of the phone with some of them. They considered her something of a curiosity now that she had left the bright lights behind, and she considered them a little dysfunctional to be so wrapped up in making money, even though she could wryly admit that she had numbered one of them only a matter of a couple of months ago.

'And these friends…are they male or female?'

'Both,' Sara said lightly. 'A bit like yours, I expect.'

'I don't encourage female friendships.' James rested the wine glass on the kitchen table so that he could link his fingers behind his head. From this angle, he could inspect her every movement with lazy, leisurely concentration. 'I find even the most dispassionate female friend usually ends up wanting more than I can give.'

'You're not as irresistible as you think you are,' Sara informed him. She hadn't done a starter, favouring a pudding instead, and now she began bringing dishes to the table and telling him what he would be eating.

James listened politely, sat squarely in front of his plate, allowed her to dish out a little of everything for him.

'Are you telling me that *you* don't find me irresistible?'

'I think we understand one another,' Sara told him lightly. 'We both know what we want out of this relationship.' In his case, sex and her house, in her case love, marriage, babies, the whole fairy tale that experience should have warned her didn't exist. Fortunately, he wasn't going to find that out.

'Which is?'

'You know what. Fun.'

'And your need to exorcise your demons.'

'Meaning?'

'Your ex-lover.' It shouldn't have bothered him. After all, wasn't he getting what he wanted? To bed the woman sitting opposite him and eating with the composed air of a saint? It bothered him like hell.

Sara shrugged and let him assume.

'Simon enjoyed today,' she said, into the tense little silence that had greeted her non-answer.

'So did I.' He paused. 'Do I hear a *but* coming…?'

'But,' Sara said obligingly, 'I really don't want a repeat performance.'

'Meaning what exactly?'

'Meaning that, while I appreciate your efforts, I don't want you to get involved with my son.'

'Why is that?'

'Do you have to keep asking questions? Can't you just accept what I tell you at face value?' She closed her knife and fork. She had been able to eat only a fraction of what was on her plate. Her appetite seemed to have done a runner.

'I've never been a great believer in accepting things at face value. There's always a deeper agenda.'

Something, she thought, he would know a lot about, considering his agenda.

'OK. The deeper agenda is that I don't want Simon getting attached to someone who isn't going to be around for very long.'

James wasn't about to let that one go. 'The dinner was delicious,' he said carefully, sitting back and folding his arms with an expression that could stop a leopard at twelve paces. 'I take it from your remark that you've already assigned a time limit to us?'

'No, of course not...'

'Simon benefits from having a man around occasionally. I'm not about to try and step into his father's footsteps, although from what you tell me that wouldn't be very difficult considering the kitchen table we're sitting at is capable of more paternal feelings. But...'

'There are no buts, James,' Sara said sharply. 'If you don't like the situation then you can clear off.' Every word was like having a knife dragged through her heart. She could feel her eyes beginning to water and hastily stood up so that she could focus on something other than his gimlet-like, narrowed stare.

'This isn't getting us anywhere.' The low murmur came from closer to her than she had expected. With her back to him, belligerently attacking the plates into a state of cleanliness, she had been unaware of his approach.

Frankly, his response alarmed her. Hadn't she just given him the perfect opportunity for a fight? She knew him well enough by now to know that he wasn't the sort of man who tolerated female attacks with equanimity, so why was he not ramming home his point?

Sara felt his arms slide around her waist and she stiffened, then began to melt.

One touch. That was all it took. When he bent to rest his mouth against the nape of her neck, she felt the bones in her body soften.

'If you feel that strongly, then of course I won't try and barge in on your little nuclear family.' Somehow he made that sound as though it was a criticism of her but she was losing the will to fight because his teeth were now gently nipping the side of her neck and making her legs feel very shaky in the process.

'Is that why you've been dodging me during the day whenever I've been down?' he murmured, reaching forward to switch off the tap and then replacing his hand a little further up her torso, beneath her left breast, in fact. 'It's perfectly understandable.'

Sara made a concerted effort to shift herself around, which she managed to do successfully, only to find that his long, lean body had no intention of moving. He kissed the tip of her nose. Then very gently kissed her mouth.

Why, why, why? Why couldn't he help her along and be as predictable as every other man on the face of the earth? *Because if he was,* she thought to herself, *then you wouldn't have fallen head over heels in love with him.* Nor would she still be falling, even though she knew full well what he was about.

She heaved a small sigh of resignation and coiled her arms around his neck, drawing him down so that his gentle kiss could be replaced by her more urgent one.

Wrong response. Definitely not in accordance with her well-thought-out plans. Definitely not a sensible manoeuvre when it came to protecting her vulnerable heart.

'I've made pudding,' she managed to protest.

'It. Can. Wait.' He punctuated the three words with hungry kisses. When he strode towards the kitchen door and slipped the latch down, all Sara could do was wait in the familiar nervous excitement for him to be back close to her.

'Now,' he murmured, pulling her to him and winding his fingers into her hair, 'I can think of a hundred more pleasurable things we can do than argue.' He smiled slowly. 'Well, only one, as a matter of fact, but that can be done in a hundred different ways, mm?'

Not a hundred, as it turned out. In fact, the kitchen proved the venue for the appetiser only and Sara had never before imagined that a kitchen table could be that satisfying an instrument in lovemaking.

Her floaty dress, which she had worn as an armour against his advances, didn't stand a chance. Not that he removed it. Just pushed it up to her waist, where it bunched around her, leaving him free to tug down her underwear so that he could explore the honeyed moisture between her legs. If the floaty dress didn't stand a chance, then neither did she, when it came to his ability to arouse her. All she could do was lie back, her head flung over the back of the chair, and enjoy his full attention.

She didn't want to come, fought against it, but the insistent flicking of his tongue against her sensitised bud proved too great a stimulation to resist and the waves of pleasure rushing through her in rapid succession left her moaning and writhing until she shuddered to her explosive orgasm.

Afterwards, face flushed, she lay limply with her dress still inelegantly at her waist, breathing heavily.

'Delicious dessert,' James murmured with a wicked smile and Sara looked at him drowsily.

'That's the corniest line I've ever heard.' She smiled back and ran her fingers lightly through his hair. He was still squatting in front of her parted legs and he placed a very tender kiss right there.

'Now, shall we go backwards?'

'Go backwards?'

'Enjoy some main course...'

For which the sitting room, with its big, soft sofa, proved just the right place. The curtains were open and the light was fading but there was still enough to bathe the room in a dusky, mellow hue. Through the French doors, the rolling scenery made her feel as though they were making love out in the open.

'Simon's upstairs, sleeping,' Sara said feebly.

'And we're downstairs, pleasuring one another. I've locked the door, so there's no need to worry, and we'll hear him anyway if he wakes up.'

This time, there were no clothes to stand between their bodies. Sara looked at him as he stood in front of her, disposing of his, and idly thought that he had a magnificent body, lean, strong, powerful and utterly lacking in self-consciousness.

And when he looked at her, he made her feel the same way. Her nudity was something she basked in and his keen eyes flicking appreciatively over her unclothed body was a massive turn-on. The fact that she had already been pleasured did not mean that he couldn't arouse her again. And again and again.

Afterwards, while Sara lay supine on the sofa, James strolled across to the French doors and closed the curtains, then he switched on one of the table lamps.

'What about the pudding I've slaved over?' she teased contentedly, looking up at him as he stood over her. She yawned and stretched and he smiled at her. A vision of absolute satisfied fulfilment. He could stay there forever feasting his eyes on her smooth, pale body, watching the way her breasts moved when she raised her arms above her head so that the pink nipples were large circles beckoning him.

'You stay right where you are.' He began shoving on some clothes, just boxer shorts and trousers and, as an afterthought, his shirt, which he didn't bother to button.

'Don't be silly, you're the guest.' But she just stretched again, languidly, and raised her heavy eyes to his.

'Which, of course, means,' he drawled with lazy intent, 'that you have to make sure that I'm one hundred per cent satisfied, and you can stay right there and think of all the ways you can do that. In the meantime, I shall fetch us both our dessert, *mademoiselle,* just so long as you tell me where to find it.'

'Larder. Just some iced brownies, I'm afraid. I'm lousy at desserts.' But what joy having him fetch them for her. There was a throw on one of the chairs, and she really should cover herself with it, but the effort involved seemed a little bit too much. Besides, and she revelled in this thought, wouldn't he just tear it off her the minute he returned?

She was aware of him returning even before he re-entered the room with the plate of brownies in one hand and two glasses of wine precariously in the other.

Sara propped herself up on her elbow and surveyed him as he deposited the wine on the table in front of them, then sat on the sofa by her, depressing it with his weight.

He dipped his finger into some icing and held the finger out to her lips, which she proceeded to suck with her eyes tantalisingly fastened on his.

'Good?'

Sara nodded.

'Well, I'd better try some for myself, in that case.' At which he repeated the exercise, but instead of proferring his finger to his own mouth he spread a sample on one of her nipples and then...oh...she could only moan as he licked it off very thoroughly before doing the same with the other aching nipple.

She was like a cat being stroked and stretching itself to its fullest so that the stroking could last forever.

Forever.

James didn't pause in his ministrations of her eager body. The realisation crept over him and it was something that he had known for a while.

Forever.

It was a good place to be.

CHAPTER NINE

JAMES sat at his desk, his long legs stretched out in front of him, planted solidly on the shiny, polished surface. At least he knew that there would be no interruptions of any kind. Everyone had gone home. He had all the time in the world to reflect. Shame that the reflections were of such a sordid nature, but then he had had ample time to consider that it served him right.

From the minute he had laid eyes on Sara King, he had stupidly thrown all his natural caution to the winds. Even when she had spun him her pathetic little story about not wanting him around because she wasn't prepared to have an affair, he had gone, only to return the minute she had crooked her finger. And how his stupidity had returned to bite him.

He looked coldly at the small black and gold bag burning a hole on the desk. Thinking about the ring inside only made him more enraged, but, like Sisyphus toiling up the mountain, it seemed that he had no choice but to stare at it and grimly acknowledge his misplaced trust.

Of course, he would have to deal with it. He had been played for a fool and he had no intention of allowing her the luxury of thinking that she had got away with it.

He swung his long legs from the desk and within minutes he was on the phone, making arrangements with his pilot for his flight up to Scotland. Then he slipped the bag into his jacket pocket. Touching it made him grimace with distaste but he almost enjoyed the feeling of repulsion because it was a strong and necessary reminder of the fact that he had been taken for a fool.

The helicopter would leave in an hour and a half. By the time he made it up to the Highlands, it would be after ten. His mother would probably be asleep. He hadn't told her that he would be arriving a day ahead of schedule. He hadn't known it himself, not until this afternoon.

If he had any sense, he would leave the inevitable meeting with Sara until the morning, but he wasn't feeling sensible. Besides, he told himself, she would have Simon around in the morning. The minute she realised that he was on to her she would hide behind her son, knowing full well that a full-blown argument would then be out of the question. And James felt ripe for a full-blown argument.

Far from calming him, the flight up gave him a little more time for his rage to intensify.

His mind wandered back to the conversation he had had with Lucy Campbell, who had called him at work simply on the spur of the moment because she happened to be in London. They had had lunch at one of the trendier places that Lucy adored because they gave her the opportunity to look at people and know that they were looking at her.

Lord knew, he would never have found out about the conversation she had had with Sara but a couple of glasses of wine had put her in a mellow mood, and, from teasing him about the fact that the Rectory had passed him by, she had confided that she had explained his desire to get his hands on it to the current owner, just, she had admitted sheepishly, to see her reaction. Jealousy pure and simple, she had admitted airily. After all, hadn't *she* been after the biggest fish in town for most of her years? But, now she had got herself a boyfriend with whom she was head over heels, she could be open and honest.

It had taken him only a matter of seconds to work out why Sara had suddenly decided, out of the blue, to get in touch with him, to throw herself at him. Revenge through seduction. He didn't care what her reasons had been. All he could feel was his own raw pain and all he could think was that he had been on the brink of proposing marriage, of becoming the vulnerable idiot once again.

Vulnerable. Idiot. Two words that had never before entered his vocabulary, or anyone else's for that matter, when it came to describing him.

As predicted, it was almost a quarter past ten by the time the helicopter touched down on the estate and getting on for ten-thirty when his car pulled up outside the Rectory.

He hadn't even bothered to go into the manor. Instead he had gone straight from helicopter to car, with his brief-case slung into the back seat.

As he had half expected, the lights were out at the Rectory. If she was up in bed she probably wouldn't hear him banging on the kitchen door, so he went to the front door instead and kept his fingers depressed on the bell until he heard the shuffle of footsteps. There was no peephole in the door. The Rectory had never been updated to include such modern conveniences. There was, however, a key chain and she opened the door just enough for him to see her peering out at him with a frown. The frown turned to delighted surprise.

Tousled red hair streaming down her back, eyes still drowsy but sexily so, mouth curving into a smile of greeting as she unlatched the door. It all added up to a woman eagerly pleased to see her man unexpectedly.

The woman should go into acting. She would be a natural candidate for an Oscar.

He wondered whether she had simulated pleasure when

they had made love as well or had she ground her teeth together and stuck it out because, at the end of the day, all she wanted was a chance to pay him back?

It galled him to think that, as he followed her into the kitchen, he was still half hoping that his conclusions had all been wildly off course.

'What on earth are you doing here, James?' she tossed over her shoulder. 'I thought you were supposed to be flying in tomorrow.'

'My business dinner was cancelled so I thought I might as well come a few hours earlier than planned. Pleased to see me?' He revelled masochistically in the need to hear her beautiful lips formulate their ready lies. She didn't let him down. In fact, she swung around and wound her arms around his neck so that she could draw him towards her, and instead of pulling back he attacked her mouth with an aggression that startled her. Though not for long. If she could fake passion then she did it very well, he thought, because her mouth almost immediately responded to his urgent plunder and her body curved against his. He could feel himself get hard in response and he roughly pushed her away.

Oh, no. Not tonight. Sex was definitely not on the menu tonight.

'Were you sleeping?' he asked, leading the way to the kitchen so that she was obliged to fall in step with him.

'What's wrong?'

James turned around to find her staring at him from the door, a small frown replacing her earlier expression of delight.

'Wrong?'

'You seem a little…strange.'

'Must be the stress of work,' he lied smoothly, watching her watching him. She was just a little too observant for

his liking and it irked him to realise that she possessed,
unusually for a woman or at least any of the women he
had ever slept with, a talent for reading his moods.

She seemed to accept the explanation, at least for the
moment, and filled the gap by chatting about what she had
been up to. Buying school uniforms for Simon, getting to
meet a few more of the local women her own age at an
informal coffee morning for some of the mums at the
school, trying to bake a cake and oh, she had bought six
chickens and intended to have farm-fresh eggs every day.

James listened to this saga of rural contentment without
saying anything. Eventually, Sara's voice dwindled away
and the silence was not the kind she had become used to
with him. It wasn't the companionable silence they always
shared. This quiet had an edge to it and it frightened her.

'Why is work so stressful at the moment?' she asked,
searching for the most obvious explanation for his peculiar
behaviour. She must be imagining it, of course, because
why else would he have come to see her at this time of
the night if not to be relaxed in her company?

'Work is always stressful.' He had made a pot of coffee
and he handed her a cup, removing himself to the opposite
end of the kitchen table, from which he could inspect her
from a relative distance. 'Didn't you find that when you
worked in London?'

'Well, yes.' She tried a bright smile but it felt worn at
the edges. It was late, even though she no longer felt tired,
and the expression on his face was disturbing her at some
indefinable level. 'But then with a child in tow, life tends
to be stressful at the best of times.' More silence in need
of filling. And not a move to touch her. By now they would
normally be all over one another, unable to stop themselves from touching, like teenagers exploring one another

for the first time instead of two adults who had already made love more times than she could remember.

'So, living here must be a dream come true.' He shot her a cool smile and noted with satisfaction the dampening effect it had. The lovely mouth began to droop and her eyes took on a guarded wariness that still had some power, infuriatingly, to pierce the part of him that he had galvanised into self-mending.

'I'm not sure about a dream come true,' Sara said with a hesitant smile. 'But yes, there's a certain magic that I would never have believed to exist when we first arrived.'

'No?'

For some reason she had never confessed the immediate dislike she had felt for the place when she had first arrived. Hiding away in the Rectory rather than going into the town now seemed like a distant dream. Perhaps she had shied away from that little admission because to insult the Highlands would have been to insult him. And then later, she found that she couldn't.

But now she felt uncomfortably goaded into rambling on.

'I guess it was such an enormous change from London. Well, you of all people must know what I mean, but then it's always been different for you because you've always lived here.' Now she could hardly believe she had stuck it out in London for so long, and with Simon as well. Mad. 'When I first came up, well, I was convinced that I'd done the wrong thing. It had seemed like fate when I found out that I'd been gifted this place and I grabbed hold of the opportunity with both hands, but leaving London was a wrench. I'd become accustomed to the noises and the chaos and the way that everything was lived in the fast lane. Always. A bit like your mum must have felt when she moved up here.'

Mention of his mother made his lips thin. His dear *mama* was not going to like this turn of events. She had developed a great deal of affection for Simon and for Sara too, come to that. Her pointedly tactful silence on the subject of her son finally finding the woman of his dreams was proof galore that that very prospect had been running through her head.

'Course, Simon adores it up here.' She was wittering. She nervously gulped some of her coffee and wondered whether he would take up the conversation if she remained silent or whether he would just sit there, with that disconcerting, forbidding expression on his face, until she began wittering again.

'So you've said before.'

'I'm sorry. Repeating myself. Must be getting old.'

Silence.

'I wish you'd tell me what's wrong.' The plea was wrenched out of her and she laughed to conceal the fear that was beginning to consume her. Fear of what, though?

'Guess who I saw today.'

'I don't know. Tell me.'

'Lucy Campbell. You remember her, don't you? It would appear that the two of you have met. Small, attractive blonde given to gossip.' He sipped some coffee and watched her face as she digested this piece of information.

'Small, attractive blonde.' So this was where it was leading. His unexpected appearance at her house, his brooding expression, the way he was making very sure not to come too close to her. He was ending their affair, if that was what it was. The fact that she had intended to be the one doing the ending never occurred to her. She had lost sight of her original plan to use him the way he had used her. All she could think of now was the prospect of never seeing him again. No more shared laughter, no more of his dry teasing, no more of that wonderful feeling of waiting for him to knock on her door, no more losing herself in their lovemaking, thinking everything was all right in the world.

He had found someone else just as Phillip had found someone else, though strangely losing Phillip had been nothing compared to what she felt now, even though he had fathered their son in the course of their brief, doomed relationship.

'Yes, I believe I do remember her, now that you mention it.' The clever girl had spilled the beans about his plans to buy the Rectory from under her feet, and look at that, she had got her man in the end.

'I thought you might.'

'Well,' Sara stood up and carried her cup to the sink then she remained there, with her back pressed against the counter and her hands splayed out on either side of her, 'you really needn't have rushed over here to tell me, James. Couldn't it have waited until morning? These things happen, after all, don't they?' She shrugged and lowered her eyes for a second.

'What things?'

'I suppose you two were destined for a life together from an early age. Isn't that how it works in this part of the world?'

'Arranged marriages?' His lip curled in cold distaste.

'Well, maybe not arranged but *expected*.' No room for serious interlopers to come along, although she had never been a serious interloper, had she? They had never talked about commitment or a future together, and he had certainly never mentioned the love word.

'Two mothers making plans for their little toddlers crawling around on the ground together? The perfect match of children with similar backgrounds, used to similar lifestyles…' She felt tears of self-pity pricking the backs of her eyelids. Different place, same old story. The daughter of a market trader should never dare hope for the impossible with a man like James Dalgleish. Ditched by two men for basically the same reason. Must be some sort of record.

'You insult my mother,' he said coldly. 'You also seem to forget that she came here as an outsider so the thought of marrying me off at the age of four to a suitable local girl would never have occurred to her. Nor am I the sort of man,' he laughed shortly, 'to meekly marry a woman because she fulfils the right criteria, even though there's a lot to be said for an arrangement of that nature.'

His words should have filled her with relief but they didn't because his expression hadn't softened.

'Besides,' he added silkily, 'Lucy has found herself a man and from all accounts she's madly in love.'

'Oh. That's nice…' Now she was confused.

'Isn't it?' He pushed his chair back so that he could stretch out his legs in front of him and afford himself a wonderful view of the apprehensive woman still glued to the kitchen sink counter. 'Although, of course, she *was* carrying a torch for me when you last spoke to her…now, what *was* it you talked about?'

'I…I don't remember.'

'That I find hard to believe.' He raised his eyebrows in a mimicry of incredulous disbelief and Sara suddenly felt like a rabbit trapped in the headlights of an oncoming car. An oncoming car that was fully aware of its existence but determined not to stop. 'You must have a memory like a knife. Part and parcel of the training you would have gone through for that job of yours.'

'I wish you'd stop playing games. Just tell me what's going on. Why did you come here so late? To tell me that a woman I met once has got a boyfriend? I can't think that sharing that piece of information really necessitated a drive here at ten-thirty in the evening!'

Her cheeks were flushed and he could see the confusion in her eyes.

Maybe, he caught himself thinking, he had been wrong about her. Maybe he had added two and two together and arrived at five.

'She told you that I had wanted the Rectory for years.' He saw the confusion in her glorious eyes cloud over with sudden guilt and the response was damning. 'Didn't she?' He smiled coldly when she didn't answer so he continued with his inexorable monologue. 'And naturally you assumed that the reason I had shown interest in you was that I wanted something from you. Please, feel free to contradict me at any point.'

'Why didn't you tell me from the beginning that you were interested in buying my house?' Her heart was hammering. Let him shower her with accusations. She wasn't going to sit down and play the easy victim.

He flushed darkly, grudgingly admiring her ability to toss his argument right back in his face. Which didn't excuse her behaviour, he reminded himself. She'd used him and what really filled him with self-disgust was the fact that he allowed himself to be used because he couldn't keep his hands off her, because he enjoyed her company, because he became addicted to it until all that rubbish about marital bliss and happy-ever-after stories ended up scrambling his very sharp brain.

'Maybe I met you and decided that the owner was more important than the bricks and mortar.'

Sara laughed a little hysterically.

How had all this gone so disastrously wrong? Three hours ago she was dishing out fish fingers for her son and happily contemplating seeing the man who was now shooting her down in flames.

'Or maybe you just decided that it would be easier to get what you wanted if you strung me along!'

'Is that when you decided that two could play at that game? So after your high-principled exit from our relationship you telephoned me out of the blue so that you could restart things between us but on your agenda?' His guilt that she might have had a point in being furious with him if she had truly believed that he had sought her company for no other reason than to soft-soap her into getting what he wanted was immediately banished by her failure to deny his accusation.

He thought of the ring resting in his jacket pocket and any inclination to see her point of view was stillborn.

She had used him and he wasn't a man to be used. Not under any circumstances.

'I suppose that was my initial reason for calling you,' Sara confessed in a low voice, 'and I'm not proud of myself.' She took a deep breath and forced herself to continue. 'I don't think there's anything to be gained from revenge but you have to understand—'

'Oh, I do, do I?' James interrupted harshly. 'I think you're confusing me with someone else.'

'Could you just listen to me? For a minute?' The pleading was back in her voice but she just couldn't help it and she was desperate to clear the air, to get across *her* point of view.

'I need a drink and something a little stronger than a cup of bloody coffee.' He pushed himself off the chair, knowing full well that he really should cease this pointless debate because it wasn't going to lead anywhere. But not yet, he told himself. He just couldn't let go of it yet. It was a form of weakness and, dammit, he knew that, could have kicked himself for it, but he couldn't help himself. One stiff drink and he would clear off, shake this woman off him for good and get back to normality.

'There's some whisky in th—'

'I *know* where the whisky is. You forget what a good job you did of making me feel right at home in your house.'

He vanished towards the small utility, where she was temporarily storing her meagre supply of alcohol, and when he returned he was carrying a stubby glass containing a generous supply of the brown liquid.

He resumed his position on the chair. Inquisitor with his suspect trapped in front of him. Or at least that was how it felt to Sara.

'I know you're angry. Furious even. And I don't blame you, but *I* was pretty angry myself when I found out that you had plans for my house. I imagined that the only minor obstacle was taking care of me and, instead of being upfront and honest, you decided to take care of me in your own way.' They both had a point of view so why was it that she felt like the one who was floundering? 'I'd been through Phillip—'

'Oh, stop hiding behind your ex, using one bad relationship as an excuse to justify your behaviour.' He pelted a mouthful of drink down his throat and shot her a steely, grim look.

'I'm not hiding behind anyone! I'm just trying to explain how I felt when I decided to…to…'

'Reverse the tables? Take care of me in *your* own way?'

'I was angry and hurt.' She looked away and bit her lip to control the flood of emotion inside her.

'And put those two together and what else do you get but a little dollop of cold-blooded revenge?'

'It wasn't like that,' Sara muttered. She took a couple

of shaky steps forward to try and close the yawning chasm between them, but the expression of icy dislike stamped on his face was enough to make her swerve away until she too was back in her original position, elbows resting on the kitchen table, body urgently leaning forward.

'And what was it like?' The remainder of his drink went down his throat and he had to say that it hadn't done the trick. He didn't feel any calmer. He just felt like another one. Which he wasn't going to have because once she'd finished her pretty little speech he was out of there.

'It was…it should have been…well…I wanted to be cool and calculating and in control of the situation but…'

Against every ounce of better judgement, he found that he was waiting for her reply.

'I guess I just wasn't the kind of person who could… deal with what I had started. I…it was fun between us. I…enjoyed your company…'

'And yet you still made sure that I was kept away from Simon. Never mind all the fun and enjoyment you were having with me.'

'Stop twisting everything I say!'

'But how can I not? In the space of a couple of hours, as I sat in a wine bar in Kensington, you changed into someone else.' He gave her a look of killing contempt. 'A truly remarkable metamorphosis. However, you will excuse me if I fail to stand back in admiration.'

'I can't stop you from believing the worst of me, but you were no angel,' Sara muttered defensively under her breath. But he had said that the bricks and mortar had mattered less than the woman who lived within them. Had he meant that or had it just been his own way of making sure that he didn't put himself on a par with her? She was racked by doubt and sickened by the motives that had propelled her into the situation she now found herself in, even though those motives had been lost very early down the line.

James ignored her barely audible protest.

'And tell me, how far did the pretence go, Sara? What were you thinking when we made love? That it was all part and parcel of your plan to reel me in and then...what...confront me with my evil, wicked plan?'

'Oh, what's the use in talking about any of this?' she said wearily.

'You still haven't answered my question.'

'I don't have to answer any of your questions.'

'But you are going to.'

'Am I? Why? Because I love hearing the way you sneer at everything I have to say?'

'Because you are a woman and women have a peculiar tendency not to want anyone to leave them with a low opinion.'

'And you should know, being the master connoisseur of them.'

But not of the one that mattered. The thought left him temporarily winded, but then the formidable self-control took over once again, and he was back with the reins firmly grasped in his hands.

'I told you...when we made love...it was...' The words were coming out piecemeal and it was galling to realise that he was absolutely right about the nature of the opposite sex. Either that or he knew her well enough to predict her thoughts and impulses.

'I didn't lie in bed with you thinking nasty, vengeful thoughts.' She tilted her chin up defiantly. 'And I know you won't believe this, but my intentions in getting in touch with you might not have been...noble...but they fizzled away.'

He shrugged as though her explanation was something

he could leave or take and that stung. He wasn't even
going to try and understand. He had come to confront her
and then he would leave without a backward glance.

What had she been for him except a bit of fun? It was
all well and good for him to adopt his high-handed atti-
tude, but he didn't love her and never had. His pride might
be temporarily dented, but he would recover within hours,
while she...

James stood up and thrust his hands into his jacket pockets. Instantly he felt the bag with the little box containing
the ring inside.

Sara scrambled to her feet. It was all over and it seemed
as if it had only just begun and she didn't want him to
leave. But she wasn't going to wring her hands and beg
and not in a million years was she going to tell him that
revenge had mattered not one jot because she had fallen
in love with him.

'And how far, just out of curiosity, was this little plot
supposed to go?' He spoke with casual indifference and
mild interest.

'I told you, it wasn't a plot. I didn't spend all that time
scheming. I made a mistake, I acted the way I did because
I was angry and hurt, I thought you had used me, but...'

She might well not have spoken. His long fingers curled
around the small square object in his pocket and his face
hardened into a cynical sneer.

'Did you perhaps envisage that I *would fall in love with
you*?' He managed to make that sound as implausible as a
day return trip to the moon and Sara visibly winced. He
gave a bark of dangerous, unpleasant laughter. 'Was that
the aim of the game, Sara? Did you think that you had
what it took to weave a magic spell over me with a little
sexual expertise and some fluttering eyelashes?' He
watched the painful blush colour her cheeks and felt like

a swine, but the box was still sitting hot in his hand and all the anger was still there, waiting to be fanned.

'No, of course not. It…it was nothing like that…' Sara stammered but she could feel a guilty flush sting her cheeks. Guilty because her dreams had been the impossible. Yes, she *had* wanted him to propose. Now that he had voiced it, she could see with dismay right into the depths of herself and she knew that she had wanted that slice of perfection, marriage to the man she had foolishly fallen in love with. Not so she could throw it back in his face with triumph, but because she wanted to spend the rest of her life with him.

'Your face is giving you away. Shame. After your sterling performance over the past few weeks.' He began strolling towards the door and she followed him in silence.

When he reached the kitchen door, he paused to look round at her. She was white-faced. Good, he thought, but there was no thrill of victory. In fact, he felt bloody lousy considering he had vented all his anger and, he told himself, had a lucky escape.

'Unfortunately, we are certain to run into one another occasionally,' he drawled, 'unless, of course, you decide to move back to London, which is probably where you belong anyway.'

'I won't be returning to London.' Her voice was hollow with the effort of not crying. 'Simon is settled here. He's looking forward to going to school in September. And I don't belong in London any more.' Which left her with the unanswerable question of where exactly *did* she belong? She had let herself forget the mistakes of the past and at some dangerous inner level had conceived the notion that she belonged wherever James belonged.

James shrugged, one of those elegant gestures that seemed uniquely his. 'Your choice. But I'm warning you that when we do run into one another, I really would rather not have any scenes. We're just two adults who had a bit of fun and called it a day when the fun began to get a little thin on the ground.'

'And, of course, no one will think twice, will they,' Sara said quietly, 'because the fun always gets a little thin on the ground when it comes to you?'

'That's right.' He pulled open the kitchen door and noted that she had stopped a few feet away from him. She looked thoroughly battered and he hardened his jaw against the weakness of compassion. She had already given him all the answers he needed and now was the time to get out. The next time he came up to see his mother, he would make damn sure that there was a beautiful woman on his arm. Let her be under no illusion that what they had was special. That would be his little private torment and he would soon put that to bed.

'Oh,' he said casually, 'and I would rather you ceased having anything to do with my mother.'

'You can't dictate who I see and who I don't.'

'Oh, but I can and I do.' His smile was cold enough to cut through steel. 'I do not see the point of any cosy relationships between my mother and either you or your son. And I suggest you pay very close heed to my warning because if I ever come up to the Highlands and walk into my house to find you there...' he left a telling pause '...let's just say you would not like my reaction...'

Well, things couldn't get much worse, could they? He had paid his surprise visit and done what she assumed he had come to do. Namely, reduce her. He had twisted her stammered attempts at explanation, walked over her need to talk, sneered at her heartfelt apologies. Now he was telling her to keep away from his mother, with whom she had developed a warm relationship and whose fondness for Simon had been instrumental in getting him to make friends.

Without making a point or exerting any pressure, she had arranged a couple of little tea parties for some of the grandmothers of children of similar age. She was a charming, delightful woman and Sara would miss her, because she knew that she would do as James had asked.

But she wouldn't stop communications without some word of explanation and that she would do in the morning. By phone. Maria always woke up before seven, a habit that seemed to creep up with old age, she had once laughed, and James rarely wandered down before nine. He liked to read the newspapers in bed because, he had once told her, it was a luxury he could never afford when he was in London.

She tilted her chin up now and folded her arms across her chest. She might as well go out with some semblance of dignity even though she felt mortally wounded.

'Goodbye, James.'

For the briefest of seconds he hesitated, struck by the realisation that this time the goodbye was final. The hesitation was swiftly replaced by his conviction that he had done the right and only possible thing. He didn't answer. Instead he gave her a brief, mocking nod of the head and closed the door behind him.

Yes, it had all gone according to plan. He had had his full-blown argument but he was still angry. He made it to his house in five minutes flat, a record he was sure, considering the darkness of the small road and the unpredictability of the turns. He had driven like a bat out of hell.

He let himself in, relieved that the house was in silence and his mother had not been on one of her jaunts down to the kitchen to fetch herself something warm to drink, a habit which she still maintained even though there was everything in her massive bedroom to make whatever she needed without having to traverse the house in darkness.

He walked through the various rooms, discarding his jacket in the vast kitchen on a chair along the way, and headed straight for the drinks cabinet in one of the smaller of the sitting rooms.

No lover tonight, he thought cynically, but who said there wasn't peace to be found in a few glasses of very fine malt whisky?

CHAPTER TEN

WHERE was he?

Where was he?

One minute on the phone. Wasn't that what they always said? One minute on the phone, one moment of distraction and a toddler could be lying face down in a pond or climbing out of a window in an attempt to net a passing butterfly or…or…

Sara felt panic ram into her like a fist and she hurled herself up the stairs, shouting out his name, pushing open doors, racing to all his favourite places to see where he might have gone.

God, but it was only seven-thirty in the morning! He was still in his pyjamas! She herself had only slung on a pair of jeans and a T-shirt so that she could drag herself down to the kitchen after a night of absolutely no sleep whatsoever, so that she could fix him a bowl of cereal!

Nausea rose up to her throat as she checked each room, frantically looking under beds, inside cupboards, realising that there was no boy hiding underneath or within.

Then the garden.

Lord, but she cursed its hidden corners as she ran like a maniac, panting now so that when she yelled his name it was more subdued and somehow more desperate.

Think.

She forced herself to try and imagine what could have compelled him to run and where.

She had been on the phone. To Maria. Half sobbing.

Explaining everything. Wondering aloud, anguished, whether she shouldn't just return to London…

Whether she should leave Scotland behind…

Then it clicked. It was like having a charge of electricity run through her body, and in response she began to run. Out of the house and across the fields that separated the sprawling Dalgleish Manor from the Rectory.

It would be a route her son would know well. He had walked it often enough with Maria, taking the short cut that bypassed the small road. The scenic route, Maria had used to tell her, so that they could look at the flowers and the birds and a bit of wildlife before the manor house rose up before them like an impregnable fortress.

It was the only way he knew how to get there.

And as she raced across the fields, she knew that that was where he was.

He had taken himself off because the conversation she had had with Maria, one which she had conducted in front of her son, not aware that his childish brain was taking in every word, every shaky sentence, had galvanised him into flight.

She dreaded to think what the outcome would be if he *wasn't* there. If there was some part of the house or the garden which she had left unchecked, some ominous part that could house a thousand dangers to a child.

The manor was within sight before she spotted him. His bright fire-engine-red pyjamas, the fluffy bedroom slippers he had remembered to put on for once. He was carrying his teddy bear under his arm and Maria was with him, stooping down, listening to whatever he was saying.

She could barely breathe by the time she made it to where they were. Then she was sweeping him up in her arms, smothering him while he waited patiently, bemused, for her to put him back down.

Maria straightened and looked at her. 'Silly boy.' She ruffled his hair affectionately. 'Seemed to think he would be leaving today, going away from us forever, before he could find any worms or finish planting those little seeds you bought for him last week. He was worried about the chickens.' She clicked her tongue and Sara met her eyes with grateful relief.

'You're a noodle, aren't you?' Could he feel the desperation seeping out of her like sweat when she held his hand?

'You said we were going to…leave. *I heard you on the phone, Mum.*'

'I was…' Sara looked sheepishly at Maria, who obligingly took up the thread as they made their way into the house.

'Just in a foolish mood,' she murmured placatingly. 'Mummies sometimes get like that.'

Simon nodded. 'I know.'

'Shall we go home now?' Sara asked.

'Can I have a look at the trains first?'

'You're still in your pyjamas.'

'But, Mum, Teddy hasn't seen the trains. Not really. He was tired the last time I came over. He fell asleep. *Please?*'

'You can help yourself to some coffee,' Maria mouthed quietly over his head. 'Give yourself time to calm down. I know how you must be feeling,' she murmured. 'When James was young, he gave me something of a fright myself. Boys. So very different from girls, I believe.'

Sara didn't want to hear about James. Just the mention of his name made something deep inside her contract in untold pain.

Surely Maria must be aware of this? After all, Sara had confessed everything to her. Had told her how she felt, poured it all out, and it had been like a swell of water bursting through a dam.

Yet…she found herself clinging on like a fool to whatever his mother had to say, anything that might break through the barrier of nothingness that had gripped her since James had stalked out the night before.

'He ran away, you know,' she was saying, bustling in the kitchen now and pouring Simon a glass of squash. It was a drink that she had never kept in the house before and it touched Sara to realise that she now stocked it, in preparation for whenever her little part-time charge might come around.

'He could only have been six or so at the time. His father had been telling him all about the salmon fishing. Had told him that he could go too when he got a little older. Of course,' Maria smiled in fond memory, 'James thought that there was no time like the present. It took us an hour and a half before we found him and I was never so frantic in my life before.' She crossed herself and shook her head. 'Now, I will take Simon and Teddy to see the trains, and you can make some coffee for yourself. James,' she lowered her voice, 'is still sound asleep.'

Lucky old him, Sara thought miserably. How nice to be able to climb into bed and know that you were going to sink into blissful, forgetful sleep. She wondered whether she would ever be able to achieve that again.

Never, she thought hollowly. Never. Not if being here, under the same roof as him, could make her feel so acutely aware, so horribly, and against all odds, happy. Just knowing that somewhere in this vast house he was in a bed, sleeping.

The silence in the kitchen wrapped itself around her as she filled the kettle, listened to it boil, spooned coffee into a mug.

Then she sat at the kitchen table and sipped her drink and stared out at the never-ending fields in front of her.

It was almost a shame when she heard the sound of footsteps heading into the kitchen. She very nearly wished that she could have just a few more minutes on her own, to wallow in her thoughts, before Simon and the inevitable daily routine swept her up again, leaving her no time to savour her misery.

She was half standing when the abruptness of the silence broke through her thoughts and she looked up.

It was neither Maria nor Simon at the kitchen door.

'What the hell are *you* doing here!'

He looked dreadful. Sara had a fleeting moment of satisfaction to see just how awful he looked. His hair was everywhere, sticking out as though he had spent hours raking his fingers through it, and his chin was dark with stubble. More disconcertingly, he was in a dressing gown, which was loosely tied at the waist.

Then the moment was gone as she took in the hostile antagonism in his blue eyes and the cold twist of his mouth.

'I...I came over because Simon—'

'Oh, spare me.' He strode into the kitchen and poured himself a glass of water straight from the tap, which he swallowed in one long gulp.

'What do you mean, *oh, spare me*!' She shot up from the chair and faced him angrily, hands on her hips, her green eyes blazing.

'I mean, if you think that you can swan up here in an attempt to make some peace, then you're—'

'*Make some peace?* Believe me, I wouldn't be such a...such a *bloody idiot*!'

'Then what the hell are you doing here? I told you I don't want you to come near this house. How many times would you like me to repeat it?' He had felt like a zombie when he had rolled himself out of his bed in search of something to quench this horrendous thirst of his. The whisky consumption had ended up being rather more enthusiastic than he had intended. He had slung on a dressing gown as an afterthought on his way out of the room. His legs had felt like jelly and his head…God, his head had been thumping.

All gone. One look at her and it was as if every muscle and nerve and pore in his body had been activated into alertness.

'If you would just stop for a minute and listen to me—'

'Listen to you? Why should I listen to you?'

'I came here because Simon is here…' Not quite the way it happened, but, dammit, the sight of him had thrown her into a state of utter confusion. She could barely get her words out, never mind put them in order so that they made sense.

'You mean you had the nerve to *bring your son up here*?' He slammed the empty glass onto the kitchen counter and Sara was surprised that it didn't shatter into a thousand pieces under the ferocity of the gesture. 'I suppose you thought that you could wheedle your way into my mother's good books? You disgust me.'

'Don't be such an egotistic idiot!' She pushed her hair away from her face and glared at him. Loving him and hating him and hating herself for feeling so invigorated even after everything that had been said and all the accusations hurled at her. Even when he was staring at her as though she was something vile that had crawled out from under a rock.

'I didn't bring Simon up here so that I might bump into you and start grovelling for forgiveness! And I didn't bring him up here to try and wheedle my way into anyone's good books! I wouldn't be here *at all* if he hadn't run away!'

'Run away!' The rampant disbelief in his voice made that sound as though, as far as excuses went, she had come up with something that hovered very near the bottom of the pile.

'That's right! I was on the phone...and when I turned around and looked for him, he was gone! I was out of my mind with worry! I only realised where he might have come when I'd searched the house from top to bottom...!'

'And why would you realise that he might have come here?'

The robe was altogether too distracting, Sara thought feverishly. She could see too much of that hard, bronzed torso and to see was to imagine a thousand things.

'Because...' She faltered, and when her eyes met his she could see the cold glitter of triumph in his blue ones.

'Because...?' He turned, poured himself another glass of water, which he downed in another long gulp, and then looked at her. 'Your little piece of fiction getting a little too involved?'

'Oh, stop it.'

She sank her head in her hands and, fool that he was, he actually wanted to go across to her, close the distance between them. His mouth tightened in self-disgust and he wondered, not for the first time, how he could have been through one catastrophic love affair all those years ago, only to repeat the experience like a child sticking his fingers into an open fire twice in succession.

Not that he had known anything about love as a young man. No, he had waited till now to fall head over heels with someone who had pulled his strings as if he had been nothing but a puppet.

'I realised he must have come here,' Sara said quietly,

raising her eyes to his, 'because I was on the phone to your mother at the time. You forget how much children take in. Simon was sitting at the kitchen table, eating his breakfast, not making a sound. I almost forgot he was there at all.'

'And what were you talking to my mother about?' He shoved himself away from the counter and moved towards her before sitting down heavily on the chair facing hers at the opposite end of the table. 'I suppose making up some lie about my role in all this? You seem particularly good at dissembling.'

'I wasn't making up any lies about anything and I'm no good at dissembling.'

'Really? I beg to differ.'

'Stop behaving as though I'm the only demon in all of this! As though you're entitled to wear a halo! You cultivated me because of what you thought you could get from me. You seduced me to—'

'To *get nothing*!' He banged his fist hard on the table and then clenched and unclenched his hands as though barely controlling an overwhelming urge to do violence. 'I might have thought at the beginning that it would be helpful to get to know you, to find out whether you intended to remain in the place…but at no point would I have gone down the road of climbing into your bed so that I could gain unfair possession to the key to your house!'

'You can't blame me for thinking that you would!'

'Because you consider me such a low form of life?'

'Because I'd been hurt once and I…' Sara drew in a deep breath and looked at him steadily. When it came to the crunch, there had been too many misunderstandings. This would be the last time she would ever have her chance to speak the utter, unadorned truth and she was going to grasp it.

'...I was foolish enough to think that I had been used again, hurt twice. Except...' He was still looking at her but there was a deathly stillness in his eyes that was draining all her courage away. 'Except what Phillip did to me didn't seem so important, not next to what you had accomplished. Because what I felt for him...look, Simon ran over here because of something I said. I told your mother that I was thinking of leaving, going back to London...he got worried.'

'You were saying about your ex-lover. I do not believe you finished your sentence.'

'You're making me nervous. I wish you wouldn't stare at me like that.'

'Where would you like me to look? At the walls? The ceiling?' His voice was scathing but his face was a study in attentiveness. It would be the last time she would command quite so much attention from him. You could hear a pin drop.

'What I felt for him was nothing like what I felt for you. Correction, *feel* for you. I was young and innocent when I got involved with Phillip and when it all went wrong, well, I thought I would never recover. When I look back on it now, I see that I recovered very quickly. I was bitter, of course, on Simon's behalf, and angry as well that he had rejected his own son, but I got on with living, working, being a mother. But with you...' She looked at him helplessly, knowing that one harsh word would release her from her need to pour everything out before they walked away from one another one last time.

But no harsh word was forthcoming and his expression revealed nothing.

'I was so utterly devastated, James, that yes, I wanted to retaliate, wanted to seduce you to teach us both a lesson. Me a lesson in not trusting and you a lesson in taking advantage of me…I didn't stop to wonder how it was that seduction should have been so easy, so pleasurable. I should have hated you, should have hated you touching me, shouldn't I? But I didn't and the reason I didn't was that I had fallen in love with you. There. Now, you can throw that back in my face, but—'

'You're in love with me.' Pure, undiluted happiness stole into his heart like a thief in the night, not that she was looking at him with the wondering eyes of a woman in love. More glaring at him, and he couldn't help himself. He smiled. A long, slow, utterly satisfied smile.

'Yes, it's funny, isn't it?' Sara snapped, springing to her feet and striding across to him, hands furiously on her hips and her hair tousled across her face. 'Positively hilarious when you think about it. So much for evening the stakes! You'll be thrilled to know that I didn't manage to achieve anything at all except to dig myself deeper into the hole I was hoping to jump out of. Hysterical. I can see you think that from the grin on your face.'

She turned to walk away, to go and get her son so that she could leave this place without completely breaking apart.

The hand that snaked out as she was swinging around, therefore, caught her unawares and this time Sara found herself falling. Again. This time literally—into his lap.

'Not so fast,' he purred and the colour rose up into her cheeks in a wash of pink.

'I've said what I wanted to say, now let me go! And you can wipe that insufferable grin off your face!'

'No, I can't. Now, tell me again. Tell me that you love me…'

'I don't intend to repeat anything for your benefit. Now *let me go*!'

'No.'

'What?' Sara struggled but it was impossible to make any headway. His arm was draped securely across her waist, just below her breasts.

And, feeble-minded idiot that she was, she couldn't help her body responding, growing hot, her nipples hardening just because she was so close to him, touching.

'I said no. I won't let you go. I want to savour this moment.' He inched his arm a bit higher so that he could stroke some hair from her face.

'It's horrible and *rude* to gloat,' she hissed.

'This is the second time you have called me rude. You will have to work on my training.'

Her response was lost as his mouth met hers, crushing every word she could utter, devouring her until she could barely remember what he had said, never mind what she had intended to ask. He kissed her ruthlessly and she weakly gave up and allowed herself to return the lethal kiss.

'Now, any more struggles and I shall have to do that again. Again and again and again. Until you hear what I have to say.'

'Which is?' She was shocked by how breathless she sounded.

'Which is that my story is very much like yours. Now, sh. Just listen, my darling.'

My darling?

'Have you been drinking?'

'Of course I have.'

'Oh.' Disappointment trickled into her, lifted when he gently kissed the corner of her drooping mouth.

'Last night. Quite a bit, in actual fact. Anything to help me get through the pain.'

Her eyes rose tentatively to meet his and what she saw there sent a flare of hope racing through her, stretching its tentacles into every bone in her body before wrapping around her rapidly beating heart.

'I told you that I had once been duped. And after that, I learnt self-control. When it came to women, they were my playthings, but I made sure never to get involved. I told myself that I was simply playing the game of relationships according to my rules. The truth was that I never met a woman who made me want to break them. Until you came along.'

Sara looked at him, mesmerised. If this was a dream, may she never wake up.

'Yes, I wanted the Rectory. And if you had been anyone but you, I would have barged in and offered to cut you a deal. A very generous deal. But you…your smile, your voice, that hesitant little way you have of looking every so often…I couldn't cut any deals. All I could do was give in to the desire to be in your company. When you made a move on me in London, everything inside was telling me to run a mile and get back to the life I used to know, where everything was under control, but I couldn't.'

'No?' Sara said stupidly, and he shook his head ruefully and smiled.

'No. You had got under my skin, lodged somewhere deep inside me, and all I wanted to do was be with you. When I realised that—'

'No, please don't say it. Please don't. I have never been sorrier or more stupid about anything in my life before.'

'I was like a wounded animal. I came back here and drank as much as I could before I lost interest in drinking and just wanted to sleep it off.'

'James.'

'Will you stay right here? Don't move. Not an inch. I'll be back in one minute. There's something I want to show you.'

He was gone literally the minute, so short a length of time that she could hardly think of what it was he wanted to show her. She was too busy basking in the euphoria of every word he had just said. She wanted to commit each syllable to heart and hold them close to her so that she could fetch them out whenever she needed to.

'This is for you.' He flicked open the lid of the black and gold box and she could only gape at the exquisite ring inside.

'But it's a ring,' she said foolishly.

'Correction. It's a ring for you, my darling. Have I rendered you speechless? Try it on. See if it fits. No, let me put it on your finger. I want to remember this moment for the rest of my life.'

'This moment…' And it did fit. Perfectly. The solitary diamond was dazzling.

'I'd intended to ask the question when I came up this weekend. I…' A dark flush spread across his cheeks and he looked like a boy, grappling to find the right words.

So beautiful. She placed her hand on the side of his face and he immediately turned it over so that he could press his lips against the palm of her hand.

'I haven't had much practice at this sort of thing…'

'Much?' Sara laughed shakily.

'Any. I just want to say that I waited all my life for you. I wish I'd known that you were right there all along, in London, with your son… My darling, will you marry me?'

'Absolutely. Yes, yes, yes. Marry you, be with you forever, live wherever you want us to live…'

'Which is right here, of course, unless…'

'Right here.' She sighed with exquisite happiness. 'Who would have thought it? Right here is where I feel I belong, next to you. Just as your mother felt being here with your dad.'

The thought was like dawn breaking over the deep blue sea. Right here. Now and forever.

Their lips met and their kiss was a seal of all eternity.

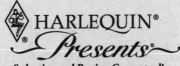

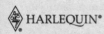

Coming Next Month

HARLEQUIN *Presents*

THE BEST HAS JUST GOTTEN BETTER!

#2481 BEDDING HIS VIRGIN MISTRESS Penny Jordan
Handsome billionaire Ricardo Salvatore is just as good at spending millions as he is at making them, and it's all for party planner Carly Carlisle. Rumor has it that the shy, and allegedly virginal, Carly is his mistress. But the critics say that Carly is just another woman after his cash....

#2482 IN THE RICH MAN'S WORLD Carol Marinelli
Budding reporter Amelia Jacobs has got an interview with billionaire Vaughan Mason. But Vaughan's not impressed by Amelia. He demands she spend a week with him, watching the master at work—the man whose ruthless tactics in the boardroom extend to the bedroom....

#2483 BOUGHT: ONE BRIDE Miranda Lee
Richard Crawford is rich, successful and thinking of his next acquisition—he wants a wife, but he doesn't want to fall in love. Holly Greenaway is the perfect candidate—a sweet, pretty florist with her livelihood in peril. Surely Richard can buy and possess her without letting his emotions get involved?

#2484 BLACKMAILED INTO MARRIAGE Lucy Monroe
Lia had rejected her aristocratic family, but now she needs their help. Their response is to sell her to the highest bidder, Damian Marquez, who wants Lia to provide him with an heir! As the wedding night looms, Lia knows the truth will out—she can't be his in the marriage bed....

#2485 THE SHEIKH'S CAPTIVE BRIDE Susan Stephens
After one passionate night, Lucy is the mother of Sheikh Kahlil's son, and if he is to inherit the kingdom of Abadan she must marry Kahlil! Lucy is both appalled by the idea of marrying the arrogant sheikh and overwhelmed by the attraction between them.

#2486 THE ITALIAN BOSS'S SECRET CHILD Trish Morey
At a masked ball, Damien DeLuca is swept away by a veiled beauty and the evening culminates in an explosive encounter. Philly Summers recognized her gorgeous Italian boss instantly—he's been invading her dreams for weeks. But she will keep her own identity secret!

HPCNM0705